Shady Shot by My Secret Baby Daddy

An Enemies to Lovers Brother's Best Friend Romance

LIVVY STONE

Contents

Join Livvy Stone's Readers' Circle!

SNAG *THOUSANDS* OF FREEBIES, bargains and sneak peeks, get the scoop on the latest releases, and be the first to dive into upcoming stories. Oh, and did we mention your welcome gift? Say hello to 'Pucking My Brother's Best Friend,' Livvy's FREE eBook crafted just for you!

Scan this QR code to join and download your free book!

Scan me

1

Zoe

"Hey there, Agent-in-Training! About time you showed up!"

My brother Ben's voice booms over the chatter as I step into his sprawling backyard, the unmistakable strains of The Weeknd's "Blinding Lights" pulsing through the air.

The scent of sizzling burgers and smoky ribs wafts from the grill. Kids dart between tables draped in red and white checkered cloths, laughter mingling with the occasional pop from a soda or beer can.

"You know the agency's going to snap me up fast with skills like mine," I shoot back, rolling my eyes but grinning, unable to truly ever stay mad at him.

Ben chuckles, ruffling my hair like he did when we were kids. "Yeah, yeah, just don't forget us little people when you're an official G-man. Or G-woman, I suppose."

Before I can retort, a man approaches, someone I don't recognize. He's tall and undeniably fit, with a kind of rugged handsomeness that doesn't need the backdrop of a suburban BBQ to stand out. His confident stride and the casual glance he throws around the gathering hint at ease, but not familiarity.

"This is Parker," Ben introduces, and our eyes lock. Something akin to an electric spark zips through me. "Parker, this is my sister Zoe, the future FBI superstar."

Parker's smile is warm, his eyes a piercing blue that seems to see right through me. "Nice to meet you, Zoe. I've heard a lot about you."

"Good things, I hope," I reply, feeling a flicker of something dangerous and thrilling as he laughs, the sound as inviting as the summer evening around us.

I take another glance at Parker, and damn, the man could stop traffic. His t-shirt clings just right, accentuating a physique that screams athlete, and when he catches my eye again, his smirk is like a physical touch, sparking a warmth that spirals dangerously low in my stomach.

He's got slightly messy jet-black hair. His striking blue eyes are so vivid, they almost glow against his tan, making them impossible to miss. His presence is just so strong and casually confident; it's a bit of a jolt to the system, in the best way.

For a moment, I let myself imagine him without the shirt, those same muscles exposed, the contours of his chest and abs perfectly defined under my hands. My mind drifts, picturing his skin, smooth and warm, the solid feel of his hard ass in my palms.

I wonder about the texture of his skin, the firmness of his body against mine. The thought alone is enough to make me space out, lost in the fantasy of exploring him, of feeling the weight and strength of him.

As I snap back to reality, slightly flushed and embarrassingly aware of my wandering thoughts, I realize Parker is watching me with a knowing look, his eyes glinting with amusement and maybe a hint of anticipation.

Parker points towards the grill, where the line has twisted into a comical shape, resembling more of a scribble than an orderly queue.

"I swear, that line's got more twists than a spy novel. Good luck if you're hungry now—you might get a burger by midnight."

A few chuckles ripple through the group nearby. Another guest chimes in, "Yeah, and with Ben on the grill, might want to check if it's still beef or just charcoal."

The laughter grows, and Parker tosses a cheeky grin around the group. His eyes meet mine across the yard, and he caps off the moment with a wink directed at me. Then, as smoothly as he stepped into the spotlight, he steps back, disappearing into the crowd.

Turning back to Ben, I try to realign my attention as he dives into details about his latest job promotion. "So they're finally recognizing your skills, huh?" I tease, taking a sip of the lemonade that he slipped into my hand.

Ben's chest puffs out a bit, pride lighting up his features. "Yeah, moving up to NHL senior logistics coordinator. More pay, more problems, you know?"

"That's awesome, Ben. Really." I muster a genuine smile for him, but my gaze involuntarily flickers to where Parker stands, surrounded by a group, his laughter ringing clear across the yard.

Ben catches where my interest lies. "Parker's one of the top players for the Washington Capitals. Guy's a big deal in the league."

"Really?" I feign surprise, trying to seem nonchalant even as my eyes steal another glance at Parker.

"Yeah, but he's not all clean-cut hero on the ice," Ben adds, his tone lowering conspiratorially. "Got a bit of a bad boy reputation. Not just during the games."

I raise an eyebrow, curious. "Oh?"

Ben leans closer, his voice lowering to a conspiratorial tone. "Rumor has it he's been playing the field—literally. Dating two women at the same time."

My eyes widen slightly, intrigued by the scandalous gossip. "Really? Two women?"

Ben nods with a mischievous grin. "Yep, and get this—they're twins. They know about each other, and from what I hear, they're both okay with it."

I shake my head in disbelief, unable to hide a smile. "That's... impressive, I guess."

Ben chuckles. "Impressive or reckless, depending on how you look at it. Just a warning, sis. Guys like Parker? They come with more baggage than a checked suitcase."

I chuckle, shaking my head. "Noted, big brother. Thanks for the heads-up."

The image of Parker and the twins, along with Ben's cautionary tale, swirls in my mind, adding a layer of mystery and allure to the man who had already caught my attention.

Still, there's something about him...

Ben raises an eyebrow, his voice half-teasing, half-cautionary. "Don't even think about it, Zoe. Guys like that? They're trouble."

He knows me too well.

I roll my eyes, brushing off his protective instincts with a flick of my hand. "Please, as if I have time for dating right now. I'm getting run ragged in training."

He laughs, the sound rich with brotherly affection and a hint of resignation. "Good way to be. Focus on your career, you know? We're both too young to get tied down. And don't forget that it's a big brother's job to keep his kid sister away from guys like that."

He winks, but there's an undercurrent of truth. Ben and I have always been close, and he's always looked out for me. I wouldn't have it any other way.

I excuse myself from the lively chatter and head into Ben's house, fishing my phone out of my pocket. The screen lights up with a message from my trainer at Quantico. My heart kicks up a notch as I unlock it to read a message from my superior.

You're making impressive waves already.

My lips curl into a smile as I scan the second text.

> We need your sharp eye on a case involving an illegal sports betting ring. Interested in joining the team?

My fingers fly over the keyboard.

> Absolutely, count me in.

As I hit send, a voice behind me breaks the quiet of the hallway.

It's Parker, his voice low and intense, his expression grave as he listens to the call coming through his phone. I catch snippets of the conversation—cryptic mentions of "the drop," "the package," and "making sure no one suspects."

My curiosity piqued, I discreetly linger in the hallway, pretending to check my phone as I try to make sense of what I just overheard. Parker's brow furrows, his jaw tightening briefly before he ends the call abruptly, slipping the phone back into his pocket with a sigh.

"Hey," he says, finally noticing me standing there. His smile seems forced now, his eyes guarded. "Sorry about that. Just some work stuff."

I nod, trying to hide my intrigue. "Everything okay?"

"Yeah, just some last-minute logistics for... long story for another time," he replies smoothly, but there's an edge to his tone that belies his casual words.

The moment passes, but the cryptic conversation lingers in my mind, stirring a mix of suspicion and curiosity. What was Parker involved in? And why did it seem like he was keeping secrets even here, amidst a casual backyard gathering?

"So," he says, changing topics. "Hiding from the party, or just from Ben's burger skills?"

"Actually, just stepping up my career game," I respond, slipping my phone back into my pocket. "Zoe Marshall," I extend my hand, the professional tone slightly at odds with the electricity crackling between us.

He grins, pushing off the door frame and taking a sip of his drink. Even small movements like this are precise, his body a fine-tuned machine. "Parker Sterling. So, an FBI agent and a hockey player at the same BBQ... sounds like the start of a bad joke."

"Or a good story," I counter, meeting his gaze. The air seems charged, heavy with something unspoken yet palpable, as we stand there, the noise of the BBQ muffled and distant.

Parker's smile deepens, his eyes twinkling with a mix of challenge and curiosity. "I'm betting on the good story."

Parker tosses the empty can into the nearby trash, his eyes not leaving mine. "FBI, huh? Should I be worried you're going to arrest me for any outstanding parking tickets?"

I chuckle, crossing my arms. "Only if you confess to something worse. I can't promise you'll get off easy, though. I'm known to be pretty tough."

He raises an eyebrow, his grin widening. "Is that so? How tough are we talking? Scare away all the bad guys tough, or just scare away anyone who tries to cut in line for burgers?"

"Definitely the bad guys," I retort, "But burger line cutters should watch out too. Justice is justice, after all."

Parker laughs, and the sound is unexpectedly delightful. "Fair enough. I'll make sure to stay on your good side then."

Just as I'm about to reply, my phone buzzes in my pocket. I pull it out to find another message from my superior.

> Sorry to cut your weekend short but need to meet ASAP. Just got crucial info on the betting ring. Can you come in?

I sigh, a mix of disappointment and excitement coursing through me. "Duty calls," I say, showing Parker the screen. "Looks like the bad guys won't wait for the end of a BBQ."

"That's a shame," Parker says, his voice dipping into a mock-serious tone. "I was about to challenge you to a game of backyard badminton as a true test of your reflexes."

I laugh, feeling a genuine pang of disappointment. "That would've been quite the spectacle."

As I turn to leave, Parker steps closer. "Hey, before you go—how about we try for a less interrupted meeting? Maybe drinks? I promise no badminton unless absolutely necessary."

"Deal," I reply, though my voice carries a hint of reluctance to leave. "But I really should get going."

"Hold up, Zoe," he says, capturing my attention once more.

As I turn to face him, the noise of the party dims around us, his presence magnifying. His warm fingers gently wrap around mine, and before I can come up with a witty comeback, he closes the distance.

Our lips meet in a bold, spontaneous kiss that zaps through me like lightning. It's passionate, thrilling, and feels absolutely right. When we part, we're both breathless, sharing a smile that says, "Wow, didn't see that coming."

I'm still reeling from the thrill but a flicker of concern cuts through the exhilaration. "That was... quite something," I manage to say, trying to catch my breath and gather my thoughts. "But do you always kiss strangers like that? Just on a whim?"

He chuckles, a sound that somehow makes him even more endearing yet raises my defenses. "Only when the moment feels absolutely right," he assures me, his eyes locking onto mine with a daring intensity.

"So, what does that make you?" I quip, half-teasing, half-serious. "A professional heart-stealer?"

Parker's smile softens, and he shakes his head slightly. "Only if I manage to steal yours," he replies smoothly, his voice low and a bit playful.

His grin widens. "Before you escape, how about you give me a way to track you down?" His tone is teasing, and I laugh as I enter my number into his phone.

He returns the favor, our fingers brushing lightly, sending a spark of electricity through me. "I'll call you," he promises with confidence that sends butterflies through my stomach.

With a final lingering look, I head back to find Ben by the grill.

"Got to head out, big brother," I announce, giving him a quick hug. "Duty calls."

Ben raises an eyebrow, looking past my shoulder briefly. "Everything okay?"

"Yeah, just something urgent came up with work," I explain, my mind still partly on Parker, his easy charm, and that inviting smile.

"Alright, be safe," Ben says, giving my shoulder a squeeze. "And text me when you get back to Virginia, okay?"

"Will do," I promise, pulling away and heading for my car.

As Ben walks me to the driveway, I feel my phone buzz in my purse. I recognize the distinct alert—it's Serendipity, the dating app that promises 'Mystery Matches' with 98% accuracy in finding soulmates.

The app alerts you when a potential soulmate is nearby, allowing a brief window to accept or decline the match. It doesn't reveal the other person's name or photo until both parties accept.

I hesitate, not wanting Ben to catch on that I'm using it.

Glancing back at the party, I catch Parker's figure in the distance. He's not looking at me but rather engrossed in his own phone. Could he have received the same notification? Or maybe it was one of the other players who work with Ben and are at the party?

I saw a couple of them looking in my direction. I shake my head, pushing the thought aside, as I slide into the driver's seat.

By the time Ben waves goodbye and I pull out of his driveway, the Serendipity notification has vanished. I find myself pondering several questions now: Is Parker Sterling too good to be true?

Could one of the hockey players, maybe even Parker, be my Mystery Match? The intrigue deepens as I think about the other players on Ben's team.

And what's up with those twins?

2

Parker

"STERLING, GET YOUR HEAD in the game!"

The shout comes from my left as I brace for the faceoff. I nod at my linemate, the tension palpable. The clock shows less than two minutes left, and the score is tied.

"Right behind you, man," I shout, crouching low, eyes fixed on the puck. The referee drops it, and instantly it's a flurry of sticks and skates.

"Left wing!" I call out, snagging the puck and speeding down the ice. The crowd's roar crescendos into a unified thunder. I weave through the opposing players, my teammate, Andy Davis, shouting directions.

"Parker, here!" he yells, skating into a clearing. I fake a pass to him, drawing a defenseman his way, then pivot sharply, keeping the puck. The goalie squares up to me, eyes tracking my every move.

"Thirty seconds!" Another shout, this one from the bench. Coach is on his feet, the team's hopes hanging by a thread.

I dart toward the goal, muscles straining, heart pounding. My mind flashes again to Zoe—her laugh, her fiery spirit. It's a jolt of energy, a reminder of what awaits beyond this game. But first, I have to win.

I pull back, feint to shoot, then pass instead to Davis, now open. "Now, Davis!"

He takes the shot, and as the goalie lunges to intercept, I sweep in, grabbing the rebound. "This one's mine," I grunt, tapping the puck with all the force I can muster. It slides past the goalie's outstretched glove and into the net.

The arena erupts, the sound almost deafening. I throw my arms up, skating back to my team, their cheers filling my ears. "That's how we do it!" Davis slaps my back as we huddle briefly, the game now tied.

"Thanks to you, man," I shoot back, our breaths visible in the cold air. "One more push, let's win this!"

The scoreboard flickers: Capitals up by one, less than a minute to go.

But in a bold, risky move, our coach had pulled the goalie for an extra attacker, trying to cement our lead. It's a gamble that could seal the deal or break us.

Suddenly, the puck slips past our defense, and a player from the Penguins seizes it, breaking away clear towards our empty net. My heart slams against my ribs; if he scores, it's game over, our comeback crushed.

I kick into high gear, ice spraying from my skates as I push harder than I thought possible. The crowd's shouts become a distant echo; all I hear is the thunderous beat of my own pulse.

"Parker, go!" My teammates' voices are desperate, urging me on. The Penguins' player, eyes fixed on the open net, doesn't see me gaining. His stick pulls back for the shot, and for a split second, the outcome of the game hangs in the balance.

With every ounce of strength left, I reach him just as he swings, my stick intercepting his, knocking the puck away in a spray of ice.

It skitters harmlessly to the side as the buzzer blares, echoing like a victory cry throughout the arena.

The crowd erupts, a tidal wave of cheers and applause as the reality sets in: Capitals win. My teammates swarm me, gloves and sticks thrown up in jubilation, the weight of their relief and excitement crashing into me like a physical force.

"We did it, Sterling! You freaking did it!" They're shouting, slapping my helmet, my back, engulfing me in a sea of red jerseys.

Breathing hard, I look around at the ecstatic faces of our fans, the energy in the arena almost palpable. Tonight, we snatched victory from the jaws of defeat, and as I raise my stick to the roaring crowd, I can't help but feel on top of the world.

Zoe's face flashes in my mind again, her smile from earlier today, and suddenly I'm eager for a different kind of win—drinks with her might just cap off one of the best nights of my life.

After the game, the locker room is alive with adrenaline and laughter. Towels fly, and the sound of clanking equipment mixes with the chatter of a hard-won victory. As I stash my gear, a few of the guys start planning the night's continuation.

"Hey, Sterling! We're rolling to The Puck & Pitcher for some beers. You coming?" Jeff Gray, our goalie, hollers over the locker room noise, his bag already slung over his broad shoulder.

I flash a wide grin, shaking my head. "Gotta pass tonight, fellas. I've got a hot date lined up."

A roar of teasing jeers and wolf whistles erupts from the team. "Sterling's bailing for a babe!" one of the guys shouts, lobbing a rolled-up tape my way.

"Better tell her she's scoring big, stealing you from the victory bash!" another chimes in, his laughter mixing with the others.

"You know it, boys!" I call back, giving them a salute as I grab my keys. "Throw back a cold one for me!" I add, heading for the exit amid their continued ribbing and chuckles.

The drive home is a blur, the streets of the city whizzing by as excitement courses through me. Tonight's game was a rush, but the thought of seeing Zoe again sends a different kind of thrill through me.

I pull into my apartment complex, still buzzing with energy, and head up to my place. As I turn the corner, my steps falter.

There, waiting by my door, is a figure I recognize instantly—a familiar face I hoped not to see anytime soon.

My heart sinks a bit, the night's high fading as I brace myself for what's next.

As I round the corner to my apartment, there they are—Damon Lacroix, slick as an oil spill in his too-perfect suit, and his personal mountain of a man, standing guard like he's outside a nightclub. Damon, with that greasy charm of his, flashes a grin that's probably insured for more than my car.

"Parker, my man, glad I caught you," he purrs, as if we're old buddies catching up over beers instead of whatever shady proposal he's cooked up this time.

"Damon," I greet him, keeping my voice cool. "To what do I owe the pleasure?"

His smile widens as he plays with his cufflinks, a little show of his obvious wealth.

"I'm sure you've been giving some thought to our recent conversation. About enhancing your financial portfolio through some friendly wagers."

I lean against my door, arms crossed. "Like I've said before, I might throw down on a basketball game or something. But I keep it clean with hockey, always."

"But Parker," he croons, stepping closer, his voice smooth as if he's trying to sell me a stolen Rolex, "imagine just amping up the fun you're already having. You know the game, you know the plays. Just a little side bet on games you know you're gonna slam. It's practically free money."

I shake my head, trying not to laugh at the absurdity. "Damon, you're barking up the wrong tree. I play to win, sure, but I do it clean. I'm not looking to score cash on the side like that."

Undeterred, Damon reaches into his coat like a magician pulling out a rabbit, but what he's got is a sleek black envelope. He offers it to me with that scheming grin. "No pressure, my friend. Just take a look. No strings attached," he insists.

Reluctantly, I take the envelope. "Inside, you'll find a few... incentives. Consider it a welcome gift, should you decide to join us," he adds, his eyes glinting with something I don't quite trust.

With a flourish, he steps back, nods to his human wall, and they both start to leave. "Think about it, Parker. Opportunities like this don't come every day."

Watching them disappear down the hallway, I flip the envelope in my hand, feeling the weight of the decision inside. Damon's offer is tempting, sure, but diving into those waters might be swimming with sharks. And I'm not sure I'm ready to get bitten.

I step into my apartment, a slice of luxury high above the city with panoramic windows offering a view of the Capitol's twinkling lights. The place is sleek, modern, with minimalist furniture that speaks more to aesthetics than comfort—a large, soft gray sectional, a glass coffee table, and abstract art on the walls that I'm pretty sure is supposed to be expensive.

The black envelope feels heavy in my hand as I toss it onto the quartz countertop of my kitchen. It lands with a slap, stark against the white surface. I eye it warily, as if it might spring open on its own and bite me.

I know I should pitch it, but after a moment, curiosity gets the better of me, and I tear it open.

Inside, there's a dossier of sorts—pages of numbers, graphs, the kind of financial temptation that could turn a saint's head. Names are redacted, but the winnings aren't, and the numbers are eye-watering. I whistle low, impressed despite myself. Tucked within the pages is a thick stack of hundreds, bound by a rubber band.

A note attached reads, "Signing bonus ;)" in a bold, confident scrawl.

Flipping through more, I find a smaller, more ominous note. It's tucked alongside information about local feds who've been poking around too close for comfort. "Don't worry—we're keeping them at a distance," it assures. My eyes catch on a name—Agent-in-training Zoe Marshall. A cold prick of dread nudges my excitement aside. *My Zoe?*

Before I can spiral too far into that thought, my phone buzzes. It's a text from Zoe, lighting up the screen with her name and a message.

> **Congrats on the win! Ready to celebrate tonight?**

A grin splits my face, slicing through the worry. Whatever this mess might be, it can wait. Tonight's about celebrating, about the rush of victory and the thrill of what might come next. I quickly type back.

> **Absolutely. Heading out now. Can't wait to see you.**

Grabbing my keys, I leave the envelope and all its implications on the counter. Tonight, it's just me, the city, and Zoe. Whatever else might be lurking in the shadows, it'll have to stay there a little longer.

I stroll into the bar like I own the place, my eyes sweeping over the crowd for a glimpse of Zoe. The buzz of conversation and the clink of glasses set the backdrop, but she's nowhere in sight. I order a drink—a bourbon, neat—and lean against the bar, my gaze still scanning the door every other second.

Just as I take my first sip, the door swings open and in she walks. Damn. If I thought she was a knockout before, tonight Zoe's in a league of her own. She's wearing a pantsuit that's all business and yet screams trouble. It's tailored to perfection, hugging her body in a way that accentuates every curve—curves that hit me square in the gut, making my pulse race. And the swell of her chest makes it a real challenge to keep my thoughts strictly gentlemanly.

Her dark hair is pulled back in a sleek, no-nonsense ponytail that somehow adds to her allure, making her hazel eyes pop—eyes that are scanning the room until they land on me. There's a softness to her heart-shaped face that belies her tough-as-nails FBI attitude, and as she makes her way over, every step is grace personified.

I straighten up, feeling a primal response kick in as she approaches. The bar fades away; it's just Zoe, moving through the crowd with an ease that speaks of power, of confidence. As she nears, I catch a whiff of her perfume, something light but intoxicating, matching the intoxicating blend of beauty and brains.

"Hey, Parker," she greets me, her voice as compelling as the rest of her.

I flash my best grin, the kind that's won more than a few hearts. "Zoe, you look absolutely stunning."

She laughs, that sound stirring something wild within me. Tonight, it's clear, is going to be anything but ordinary.

3

Zoe

"You know, I was actually a bit skeptical about going out with a hockey player," I confess, unable to suppress the smile tugging at my lips as I watch his reaction. "Jocks have never really been my type."

We're nestled into our booth, the backdrop hum of the bar wrapping around us, creating a cocoon that feels both private and charged. I'm nursing my second drink, the warmth of the whiskey mingling with the unexpected thrill of our banter.

Parker leans back, a playful smirk curling his lips as he raises an eyebrow in challenge. "Oh yeah? So, who *is* your type then?"

Laughing, I play along, swirling my drink casually. "Well, I've been pretty loyal to one guy for the last few years. His name is the FBI," I tease, keeping my tone light but my eyes fixed on his, gauging his response. "He's demanding, never boring, and keeps me up at night."

"Sounds like a tough guy to compete with," Parker replies, the edge in his voice making it clear he's up for the challenge.

His gaze is intense, and I can't help but let mine wander briefly—over his broad shoulders, down his thick arms, back to those piercing blue eyes. The physical pull is undeniable, and it's disarming how quickly I feel the heat rise between us.

"He is," I say. "Which is why I've totally given up on dating. He's possessive like that."

He laughs. "Totally given up? Sounds drastic. The FBI's sounding more like a convent."

I grin. "You wouldn't be too far off with that."

"So, what does 'giving up dating' entail?"

"You heard of this app, Serendipity?"

"Sure have. And believe it or not, I have it too."

"Well, I canceled my subscription and deleted it."

"Is that right?"

"That's right. No time for dating. Not to mention... I don't know, seems weird to hand something like love over to an *app*. Better to hope something happens in real life, right?"

He smirks. "You mean, like *real* serendipity?"'

I laugh. "Something like that. And a little trusting my gut while I'm at it."

The moment hangs in the air, neither of us addressing the little fact that, while I've given up dating, I'm, well, currently on a date.

His gaze locks onto mine, and I can't help but take a moment to appreciate how his powerful chest really fills out his shirt. But it's those eyes that reel me back, signaling he's more than just another handsome face.

"So, Zoe," Parker leans in, his voice carrying a hint of genuine intrigue, "I have to know, what drove you to the FBI?"

I pause, swirling the ice in my drink, weighing how deep to dive.

"Lost my mom when I was young," I start, keeping the tone light despite the heavy backstory. "My dad was a cop. Growing up around that, I saw how crucial the law is." I flash a quick, confident smile. "But local PD? Too small for me. I always aimed higher."

Parker nods, clearly impressed. "That's tough. Taking a loss and turning it into your life's mission... not just anyone can do that."

It feels good to hear that from him, acknowledging the drive it takes. "What about you? Been conquering the ice since you were in diapers?"

He chuckles, a sound that stirs something warm inside me. "Pretty much. I've had skates on since I could stand. My folks pushed me hard, but they didn't need to push too hard—I fell in love with the game all on my own."

I watch him light up as he talks about hockey, his enthusiasm infectious. He's not just a player; he's a man with a passion that matches my own ambition. Listening to him, I can't help but feel drawn in, not just to his story, but to him.

We signal the bartender for another round, the easy flow of conversation making the drinks slide down all too smoothly. I can feel the warmth of the whiskey tinting my cheeks, but I'm enjoying the buzz—it's just enough to loosen the edges.

"How do you know Ben?" I ask, genuinely curious. Parker seems to fit seamlessly into the circle of people I care about.

"He's one of the best logistics guys in the NHL—everyone knows him," Parker replies with a nod. "And he's a great guy. We've hung out a few times, nothing crazy. I mean, I'm not exactly a party dude."

I narrow my eyes, a playful smile tugging at my lips.

"Really?" I challenge, leaning forward. "Because I might have done a little digging before our date. Turns out you're a bit of a wild card, Parker. And quite the playboy, or so the internet says."

Parker laughs, the sound rich and unguarded. "What, did you run an FBI background check on me?"

I shake my head, amusement bubbling up. "Didn't need to go that far—it's all online."

He grins, unabashed. "I'm just a guy who likes to have fun, Zoe. Life's too short, you know?"

"Too short, as in *dating twins at the same time*?"

His eyes flash, and I can tell I've hit on something.

"Hoping that wasn't in the background check."

I laugh. "Nope, just good old-fashioned gossip. But still, a girl's got to wonder…"

He takes a sip of his drink, not seeming bothered. "That's why you can't trust gossip – got to go straight to the source."

"And what does the source have to say?"

"Just standard exaggerations. A couple years back, I dated a very nice model named Kim DeWitt. Tall, willowy, blonde – that sort of look."

"Go on…"

"Things didn't last. A few weeks later, I ended up hitting it off with another woman, named Shannon Saunders."

"Let me guess – another model, also *very nice*, tall, willowy, blonde, that sort of look?"

He laughs. "You've got it. But not twins – two very different women. Of course, the gossip mill added its own twist, and before too long dating two similar-looking women back-to-back became 'dating twins.' It's fun to be famous, huh?"

"Sounds like a tall tale, TMZ-style."

"Something like that. Anyway, the point is that I like to have fun. But not *that* kind of fun." Then he leans in, his eyes twinkling with a mischievous glint. "What about you? Anything to Zoe other than early mornings at the FBI shooting range?"

The directness of his flirtation sends a little thrill through me. I meet his gaze, my own smile deepening. "I've been known to cut loose from time to time," I admit, my voice low and a bit more sultry than intended.

Parker's smirk broadens at my response, the air between us charged with an exciting tension. It's clear he's really into this flirtation, and truth be told, so am I.

A strange look forms on his face.

"What's up?" I ask.

"Just thinking about Serendipity."

"You mean the app, or the actual concept?"

I smirk at his joke. "The actual thing. We both have it, right?"

"Kind of. I deleted mine, remember?"

"Right." He leans in. "Reinstall it. I want to see something."

I flick him a grin before taking out my phone. I quickly go to the app store and re-download it. Soon, the big, purple heart icon for the app is back. I tap it, and within seconds, have my account up and running.

"Now what?" I ask.

He says nothing, setting his phone down on the table.

Seconds later, it buzzes. Mine does too, my heart skipping a beat.

"Let's check," he says, raising an eyebrow.

We both do. I tap the screen, unblurring the picture of the man I'd matched with. Sure enough, it's Parker. He holds up his phone, showing me a picture of myself.

"Little did you know," he says, a smirk curling his lips. "You're not just on any date – you're out with your soulmate."

I laugh, and he does too. It's silly, but damned if it doesn't get me feeling a certain kind of way.

The evening suddenly promises even more fun than I had anticipated.

***

Back at his place, the door barely clicks shut before we're on each other. The energy from the bar, the flirtation, it all culminates the second we step over the threshold. Our kisses are hungry, desperate even, as if we're trying to make up for lost time. Our hands roam fervently, exploring each other's bodies with an urgency that's both thrilling and overwhelming.

Between breathless kisses, I manage to whisper, "I never do this," my voice shaky, not entirely sure whether I'm trying to convince him or myself.

"Sure, sure," he murmurs back with a grin, not slowing down for a second. His tone is teasing, light, but there's a sincerity in his eyes that tells me he's just as caught up in this as I am.

Suddenly, his phone rings. He stops, tearing himself away from the kiss and slipping his phone out of his pocket.

He winces as he looks at the screen. "Sorry, I *really* have to take this – should just be a sec."

"No problem."

He leans in and kisses me. "Hold that though, OK?"

With that, he hurries out of the other room. "You got the package?"

The package. My mind flicks back to that conversation at the party, the weird one about dropping something off.

This time, my curiosity isn't staying on the sidelines. I tiptoe after him as he steps into the next room to take the call, leaving the door just a crack open.

"Yeah, everything's set for the surprise," I hear him say, his voice bubbling with excitement. "No, he has no idea. It's going to be great. Yep, during the third period break right on the ice. Make sure the Zamboni is decked out for the occasion, okay?"

The pieces fall into place. No shady dealings here, just Parker setting up a surprise bash for someone. When he hangs up and steps out, I can't help but wear a smirk.

"Got a little party planned on the ice, huh?"

Parker, caught off guard but relieved, chuckles. "Yeah, it's Gary, the Zamboni driver's retirement party. Wanted it to be a surprise—something special during the game. And we got him a little care package of some cupcakes our forward's wife made for him."

I grin. "That's really sweet, Parker. A Zamboni send-off?"

"Yeah, Gary's going to lose it." He matches my grin with one of his own. "Speaking of *losing it*, that's what I'm going to do if I don't kiss you again."

"Then get over here and do it."

Just like that, our lips are locked again.

I can't believe I'm ready to sleep with him, barely hours after our first real date, but there's something about Parker. Something that pulls me in, makes me want to forget all my usual reservations.

Clothes shed piece by piece, discarded carelessly around his apartment. His hands are everywhere, igniting fires wherever they touch. When his lips find their way to my breasts, his mouth warm and insistent on my nipples, a shiver runs through my entire body. The sensation is intoxicating, overwhelming, and all I can do is hold on to him, lost in the whirlwind of touch and response.

As we shed our layers in a frenzy, our banter keeps pace, electric and teasing. I catch his eyes wandering appreciatively as he unhooks my blouse.

"Are you always this thorough with your investigations?" he asks, a sly grin playing on his lips as I trace a finger down the center of his chiseled chest.

I match his grin with one of my own, stepping closer, the heat from his body mingling with mine. "Only when the subject matter is this captivating."

The more we peel away, the more I'm struck by the perfection of his physique—every muscle sculpted as if he's stepped out of some high-end fitness magazine. And damn, his butt is a work of art, perfectly firm and begging for attention, which I gladly give with a playful squeeze. He chuckles, a sound that's deeply sexy, encouraging my bold exploration.

With a sudden move, he lifts me effortlessly, a reminder of his strength. He carries me to the couch and gently sets me down, his eyes locked on mine with an intensity that makes my pussy clench. Before I know it, he's leaning in, and I'm pinned beneath him, the plush cushions barely registering beneath the weight of his presence.

His arousal is unmistakable, outlined against the fabric of his boxer-briefs. I reach down underneath the elastic of his waistband, taking hold of his cock. He's thick and hard, feeling perfect in my grasp. I move my grip along his length, reaching down all the way to his balls and giving them a light squeeze.

He lets out a low, approving growl as my hands venture to explore, stroking him through the material. His reaction is immediate and intensely satisfying. Precum forms on his end, and I waste no time using that to give my touch a better glide.

Quick to escalate the game, he deftly removes my panties, tossing them aside. His fingers dance expertly between my thighs, his touch sparking an electrifying pleasure that arcs through me. He teases me a bit before spreading my lips and thumbing my clit, the intensity ratcheting up a notch.

I arch towards him, eager and responsive, as his skilled hands drive me towards the brink, each movement deliberate, promising even more intense delights just on the horizon. He slips a finger into me, my tight wetness gripping him. It feels amazing, but a little bit of him inside of me only makes me want to feel his cock deep between my legs.

As Parker's fingers continue their masterful exploration, his voice lowers into a husky, tantalizing whisper that sends a thrill up my spine.

"You like that?" he murmurs as he finds just the right spot, his movements both teasing and deliberate. "I want to hear you say it."

Caught up in the waves of building pleasure, I can barely nod, but I manage to whisper back, "Yes, oh God, yes."

"You're so responsive, I love it," he growls, his breath hot against my ear, sending shivers through me. The sensation builds—intense and focused—until I'm on the edge, breathless and begging without shame. "I love the look on your face as you're about to come."

The man's good – he can already tell when I'm nearing my peak. He curls his finger inside, hitting my G-spot *exactly*. I gasp, bucking into his hand again.

"Just let go, Zoe," he coaxes, his voice as commanding as it is seductive. And with a few more skilled strokes, he pushes me over the edge into a blinding orgasm that washes over me in waves of intense pleasure. "Come for me. Come right now."

As I'm catching my breath, still trembling from the aftershocks, I reach for him, my hands sliding down to his waistband. I pull him free of his underwear, and my breath catches at the sight of him. His manhood is impressive—perfectly shaped, the length and girth a gorgeous testament to the rest of his toned physique.

Without wasting a moment, Parker positions himself over me, his eyes searching mine for any hesitation. "Do we need protection?" he asks, his tone serious despite the heat of the moment.

"I'm, um, clean," I assure him quickly, my voice eager, not wanting anything to delay the connection I'm craving.

He grins. "Same here. The NHL doesn't mess around with health."

And that's that.

Satisfied, he aligns himself with me, and as he glides inside, the sensation is overwhelming. The fit is perfect, filling me completely in a way that sends new waves of pleasure radiating through every nerve. His movements start slow, deliberate, each thrust deeper than the last, escalating our pleasure to heights neither of us had anticipated. The feeling is otherworldly, every sense heightened, every touch electric.

Parker's body above me is a landscape of muscle and intent. Each movement is a testament to his strength, the defined muscles of his arms and shoulders working in harmony as he moves in and out with a precision that sends sparks of pleasure shooting through me. His chest against mine feels solid, his heartbeat a rapid drum that matches the racing of my own.

I'm captivated by the sight of him, his concentrated expression as he finds the perfect rhythm. His eyes, dark blue and intent, never leave mine, deepening the connection that electrifies the space between us.

"You're doing something right, Zoe," he murmurs, his voice rough with desire. "Think you can keep up with me?" His words, a blend of challenge and invitation, spike my arousal even higher.

"Watch closely," I challenge, my voice thick with daring as I synchronize my movements with his powerful thrusts. Each push from him meets a forceful response from me, escalating our fiery dance. His tone shifts, deep and commanding, heightening the tension.

"Tell me you want it," he demands, his words laced with authority.

I shoot back, my voice a mix of defiance and desire, "Make me admit it."

His smirk is palpable in his voice, "Oh, I will. You think you can handle that?" His works send a thrill through me, urging me on.

"Yeah," I manage to say, my breath catching, "But only if you promise to make it worth my while." As the pleasure builds, it becomes almost unbearable. "Now, ask me nicely to come."

I squirm, barely able to hold a thought, let alone speak. "Please. Please let me come."

"Do it."

When the climax overtakes me, it's fierce, leaving me gasping, and I can feel Parker reaching his own breaking point. The sensation of him finishing inside me is intense—the warm flood, the ultimate connection. We find release together, and it's staggeringly perfect, a shared surrender that leaves us both shuddering.

Lingering in the afterglow, we hold each other, the room wrapped in an intimate silence that's punctuated only by our heavy breathing. It feels like we've known each other far longer than just a few hours, the depth of our connection surprising yet natural.

Our kisses are slow, lazy, the banter between us light but edged with a newfound affection. "Not bad for a hockey player," I tease, resting my head against his chest.

He laughs, his chest rumbling under my cheek. "Just trying to impress you," he says, his hand tracing lazy circles on my back. "Did it work?"

"Maybe," I reply with a playful smirk, feeling his arms pull me closer. "Might need a few more tests to be sure."

As sleep begins to pull at my consciousness, I feel secure in his embrace, comforted by his steady presence. Drifting off, I'm left with a sense of anticipation, eager to explore where this unexpected connection might lead us.

***

I wake up in the middle of the night, feeling restless. The room's dim, lit only by the soft glow of city lights sneaking through the curtains. Beside me, Parker's out cold, looking unfairly handsome even in sleep.

His chest rises and falls with each breath, peaceful and oblivious to the world. I take a moment just to watch him—the sculpted back, the arms that had held me so well, and yes, a sneak peek at his manhood, tranquil in the quiet of the night. Quite the sight, but even that masterpiece can't quench my sudden thirst for water.

I slip out of bed and pad into the kitchen, my feet cold against the tile. As I flick on the light, something catches my eye—a black envelope, casually tossed on the counter with a bit of money peeking out like a tease. It screams 'none of your business, Zoe,' but let's be honest, 'mind your own business' was never really my style, especially with my FBI senses tingling.

With a mix of curiosity and a rising alarm, I snatch the envelope, feeling its weight. Inside, the contents lay bare a sordid tale—sheets detailing illegal sports betting and thrown matches. And there, chillingly, involvement with betting rings, the very scum I've been tracking at work. The icing on this disaster cake? A list of FBI agents on the case, with my name shining bright. Perfect, just perfect.

Everything inside me turns cold. The charming man in the bedroom is tied up in everything I fight against. How's that for irony? Betrayed by the bad boy, cliché much?

I throw on my clothes in record time, each piece feeling like armor as I prepare to bolt. One last glance at Parker, so serene in his slumber, and my heart aches—a cocktail of anger, shock, and a twisted stab of longing.

I'm not done yet, however. The evidence I see here is too good to pass up. After quickly arranging the papers on the counter, I grab my phone and snap a few shots. Perfect.

As I step into the elevator, the doors close with a soft chime, like the period at the end of this very short, very messed up chapter of my life.

"Never again," I whisper to myself as I descend, the words a quiet vow in the darkness.

So much for trusting an app *and* my instincts.

I can't help but chuckle ruefully. Serendipity app, huh? Sure, it asked me about my favorite movies, my pet peeves, even my ideal Sunday morning. But not once did it think to ask, "Is your soulmate a crook?" You'd think they'd have that base covered.

Falling for a man like him? Not a chance. Not in this lifetime.

4

Parker

SIX YEARS LATER

"ALRIGHT, TEAM," I START, kneeling to be on their level, my voice taking on a tone of mock solemnity. "Believe it or not, I was about your size when I first hit the ice. So, if any of you are dreaming about playing in the big leagues like me, let me tell you—it's never too early to start chasing that puck."

Out on the ice, it's just me and this summer's squad of five-year-olds, each of them decked out in oversized jerseys and helmets that bobble with every tentative glide. They're a sight—barely able to stay upright on their skates, yet their faces are set with the determination of seasoned pros.

It's impossible not to smile at the serious intensity in their wobbly stances.

I sweep my gaze across the eager group of youngsters, their helmets nodding slightly as they hang on my words.

"Hockey's not just about being big or strong; it's about heart, passion, and practice. Lots and lots of practice. And guess what? You've already started, and that's something to be proud of."

I spot Noah, one of the kids, making faces at Charlie. "And *sportsmanship*," I say pointedly, but with a smile. "Let's not forget about that." I raise my eyebrow at Noah, who quickly gets the hint.

"Every time you step on this ice, you're getting better, even if you don't realize it. Every fall, every slip—they're all steps on the journey to becoming great players. And who knows? Maybe one of you here might even captain your own NHL team one day. Just remember, every champion was once a beginner who decided to keep going, no matter how tough it got."

I finish off with a smile, encouraging them to keep those dreams big and their sticks on the ice, hoping to ignite a spark of ambition in these budding athletes.

Ben, who's helping me run this summer hockey camp, chuckles from my right, giving the kids an encouraging nod. His presence brings a bit more authority, not that these little tykes need much corralling with their attention glued on every word I say.

Just then, a tiny hand shoots up, and a little girl with bright eyes asks, "Did you ever fall down when you started?"

I grin, nodding emphatically. "Oh, I fell down a lot. And I mean a lot. But here's the trick—every time you fall, you've just gotta hop right back up. It's just the ice's way of giving you a high-five, letting you know you're doing great."

The kids erupt into giggles, the tension in their little bodies easing as they absorb the message. Ben gives me a thumbs-up.

"Remember, every great player starts with a great fall, and then another, and probably a bunch more after that," I continue, winking at them.

The ice around us fills with laughter and the scraping sound of skates as they take the lesson to heart, a little more fearless with each slip and slide.

Wrapping up the pep talk, I throw a charming grin towards the stands where all the parents are perched, their eyes glued to the scene. "And a big shout-out to all the fantastic parents! Thanks for trusting us with your future NHL stars," I announce, my voice carrying across the ice. "We're pumped to get started tomorrow and hope you all enjoy your stay here in Maple Hollow. It's one of the best spots in Vermont, and it's going to be an epic month at our camp."

As the little troops disband, skating clumsily yet excitedly towards their families, Ben slides over to me with a big grin plastered on his face.

"Nice speech, man," Ben chuckles, giving me a nudge. "You really got a way with the kids."

"Just spreading some of that old Parker charm," I reply, watching the kids reunite with their parents, feeling a bit of pride bubble up. "Gotta give them a taste of the magic we grew up with, right?"

We make our way off the ice, stripping off our skates. Ben's still shaking his head as we head towards the lockers.

"Man, the amount of cash some of these families are dropping just to get their kids on ice with us... We're drawing folks from all across the country. Maple Hollow's turning into a national sensation faster than I can lace up my skates."

I can't help but laugh, slinging my bag over my shoulder. "Who would've thought our sleepy town would be the place to scout future hockey legends? But hey, if they keep showing up, we'll keep coaching. Champion Skates Hockey Camp is just getting started."

Striding through the corridor, our skates clacking against the floor, we're already plotting tomorrow's drills and games, ready to mold these kiddos into the next big thing on ice. The energy's infectious—looks like this summer's going to be one for the books.

As Ben and I make our way out, I toss one last wave at the cluster of parents still hanging around the stands. I can't help but notice a few wary glances thrown my way. Despite the years and the distance from my NHL days, some memories aren't so quick to fade.

Ben catches my eye and leans in, lowering his voice as we push through the rink doors. "Don't sweat it, Parks. It's been five years since the betting shit. No one cares about that anymore."

I snort, half-amused, half-bitter. "The looks on some of their faces beg to differ, buddy."

We step out into a stunning June day, the sun high and bright, casting a warm glow that should've lifted my spirits.

Ben, ever the optimist, claps me on the back. "Sure, you've got a bit of a past, but look at you now—head coach of one of the top junior hockey training camps in the country. That's what people see, that's what matters."

I squint against the sunlight, doubting. "Not sure if a good slap shot can really erase a bad slip-up in their books," I mutter, my gaze lingering on the last few families dispersing in the parking lot. "Doesn't even matter if it was something I didn't actually even do."

Ben laughs, steering me towards the car. "Trust me, Parker. Your new rep is what's making waves now, not the old news. You're shaping future stars here. That counts for a lot more than old mistakes."

As we drive away, I can't shake the mixed feelings. Sure, the camp's success is something to be proud of, but the shadow of my past is always lurking, ready to slide over the bright spots.

Ben might believe in redemption more than I do, but it's going to take more than summer sunshine and a whistle to convince me that everyone else does too.

Ben claps me on the shoulder as we head toward the parking lot. "Hey, man, you up for grabbing a drink to toast the start of the new camp? We've earned it."

I nod, eager for a bit of downtime. "Yeah, I'm in. Let's do it."

We're about to split towards our cars when Ben pauses, a look of sudden remembrance crossing his face. "Oh, almost forgot to tell you—my sister and her kid are coming into town for the training camp."

The name hangs in the air, unspoken but heavily implied. "Zoe?" I manage to choke out, my heart rate spiking.

Ben laughs, oblivious to the turmoil he's just sparked. "Yeah, who else? I don't have another sister." He gives me a quick wave before hopping into his car and driving off, leaving me standing there, stunned.

Zoe. The name echoes in my head, a vivid flashback of that night flooding back—her laughter, the heat of our connection, and the sudden chill of her departure in the early hours.

She was one of the agents involved in the investigation that eventually led to my ouster from the NHL. The irony that I'd never actually placed a bet myself, let alone thrown a damn game, didn't matter in the court of public opinion.

And there's another layer—Ben doesn't know we ever hooked up. That our brief, intense fling ended with her leaving me high and dry without a backward glance.

My stomach knots as I unlock my car. This summer, already set to be a challenge with the camp, just twisted into something even more complex. And she's got a kid? Guess a lot can happen in a few years – I'd know that better than anyone.

As I start the engine of my G Wagon, my mind races, already dreading and anticipating the inevitable collision of past and present.

This summer just got a hell of a lot more complicated.

5

Zoe

"MOM, THINK UNCLE BEN will let me skate backwards? Or show me how to slapshot?" Owen's rapid-fire questions shoot at me faster than a one-timer.

As we zip along the curvy Vermont roads, surrounded by a post-card-perfect landscape, Owen's nonstop hockey chatter fills the car. He's nearly bouncing out of his booster seat, every bit the mini puck slinger he aspires to be.

"Uncle Ben's probably gonna start with the basics, Ace," I reply, glancing at his excited reflection in the rearview mirror. "But you'll be flying across that ice in no time."

"I'm gonna learn it all! I'm gonna be the best!" he declares, pumped up like a little league superstar.

"You've got a knack for this, bud," I say, my words trailing off slightly, mindful of the father he's never known but whose talent he unknowingly mirrors.

The drive through Vermont's lush scenery is a welcome distraction as we get closer to Maple Hollow.

"We're gonna rock this summer," I tell him, reaching back and squeezing his hand reassuringly. "This is our big league debut." His grin in the mirror tells me he's all in, and as Maple Hollow comes into view, I feel a surge of that same unstoppable spirit.

As we round a gentle bend in the road, Maple Hollow reveals itself, nestled like a secret in the heart of a lush Vermont valley. With a population of a little over one thousand, it's the picture of quaint small-town charm, its beauty a stark contrast to the bustling streets of DC. The serene setting, with rolling hills cradling the town and a postcard-worthy main street, promises a peaceful escape, if only for a month.

We pull into downtown, and it's like stepping back in time. The main street is lined with beautifully maintained colonial buildings, their colorful facades hosting an array of boutique shops, cozy cafes, and even a quaint old movie theater that looks like it popped out of a 1950s film reel. Flower baskets hang from lampposts, and the sidewalks are busy with locals enjoying the sunny afternoon.

Owen presses his face against the car window, his excitement peaking as we pass an old-fashioned ice cream parlor, its cheerful striped awning fluttering in the breeze.

"Mom, look! Can we go there later?" he asks, pointing eagerly.

"Definitely, bud. First ice cream's on me," I promise, sharing in his excitement.

We continue a short distance from the bustling downtown to our Airbnb, located in a quieter, tree-lined neighborhood. The house we pull up to is a charming Cape Cod style, with a fresh coat of white paint and green shutters that perfectly complement the surrounding greenery. A small porch with a couple of rocking chairs invites relaxation, and the garden is blooming with early summer flowers.

Stepping out of the car, I take a deep breath, the fresh, pine-scented air filling my lungs.

"Here we are, big guy. Our home away from home," I announce as I unload our bags.

Owen races to the front door, his energy boundless.

As we step into the house, the charm we admired outside continues seamlessly indoors. Each room is cozy and welcoming, bathed in soft lighting and adorned with warm wood accents that give the entire place a comforting, lived-in feel.

I spot a small desk nestled in the corner of the living room, its surface bathed in natural light from a window that offers a picturesque view of the garden.

"This spot looks perfect for getting some work done," I comment, more to myself, appreciating the peaceful setting.

Owen, who's been darting around exploring each corner, pauses and gives me a pointed look.

"Mom, you promised you're not working much this month, remember?"

I laugh, ruffling his hair as he comes over. "You're right, I did say that. Guess it's all about hockey and hanging out with you, huh?"

He grins, satisfied with my response, and turns his attention back to exploring the new surroundings.

We're just starting to unpack when there's a knock at the door. Before I can even move, Owen's excitement propels him toward the sound.

"Uncle Ben!" he yells as he flings the door open.

Ben stands on the doorstep with a wide grin, opening his arms just in time to catch Owen in a big, enthusiastic hug. "Hey, champ! Look at you, all ready for hockey camp!"

I follow, smiling at their reunion. "Great to see you, big bro," I say as he steps inside.

"You too, little sis!" He comes over and gives me one of his patented bear hugs. Just wanted to make sure you two found the place okay."

Ben follows us into the living room, where Owen eagerly starts pulling out his hockey gear, laying it out piece by piece.

As Owen chatters on about the various pads and helmets, Ben and I take a seat on the couch, watching him with total amusement.

"So, how's the remote life treating you?" I ask, nodding towards the window that frames the idyllic Vermont scenery.

Ben settles into an armchair, a contented smile playing across his face. "It's been great, actually. Moving here from DC was the best decision I ever made. The job's fully remote now, so why not enjoy the peace?"

He leans forward, his tone turning persuasive. "You should consider it, Zoe. Vermont could use someone with your skills, and it's a fantastic place to raise a kid."

I laugh, shaking my head slightly. "Tempting, but you know I need to be where the action is. Whether I like it or not, DC is where I have to be."

Owen overhears and chimes in from across the room, "Can we move here, Mom? I could play hockey all the time!" His hopeful expression makes me smile, but I know it's not that simple.

"I appreciate the thought, guys," I say, turning back to Ben. "And thanks for squeezing Owen into the camp. I know it's getting popular."

Ben's smile widens, and he waves off my thanks with a dismissive hand. "Are you kidding? I'm thrilled to have my little man here. Plus, it gives us a great excuse to spend the summer together. It's a win-win."

His genuine pleasure at having us here softens the sting of my professional obligations back home.

"Remember, the camp is a few hours each day. That'll give you a little break from mom duty," he suggests with a friendly nudge. "You could catch up on work if you need to."

Owen, overhearing our conversation again, pops his head around the corner, his expression serious. "But Mom…"

I can't help but laugh, impressed by his attentiveness. "Caught me there, huh?" I ruffle his hair as he comes closer. "Don't worry, buddy, I'm on vacation time. Your uncle is just making sure I remember how to relax."

Ben chuckles, then shifts the topic. "So, how's life at the agency going? Still keeping the world safe?"

I sigh, my shoulders dropping a bit with the weight of the question. "Honestly, while I love doing good, it can be pretty grim work. Not to mention it doesn't leave much time for this guy," I say, nodding towards Owen.

Ben's expression softens. "Well, then, this month will be a good chance to catch up on all that, Zoe. Take a breather from everything. Maple Hollow's a good place for slowing down and just enjoying life."

His words resonate with me more than I expected.

Ben pops up from his seat, stretching a bit as he readies to leave. "Alright, I'll leave you guys to settle in. How about I come back later and take you out for pizza? There's a spot downtown that's out of this world," he suggests with a wink.

Owen beams with excitement. "Pizza? Yes, please! Can we go, Mom? Then ice cream?"

"Absolutely," I respond, thankful for Ben's knack for keeping things light and fun.

"Perfect! Oh, and we'll meet up with the other guy running the camp with me. You haven't met him yet," Ben adds as he grabs the doorknob.

Curiosity piqued, I follow him to the door. "He's a former hockey player, right?" I recall Ben mentioning something along those lines before.

"Yeah, that's right. Name's Parker Sterling, used to light up the ice for Washington," Ben says, throwing a casual glance back at me.

The name hits me like a truck. Parker Sterling. My heart does a dubious flip, and I feel a chill despite the warm Vermont air. Of all people, Parker was the last I expected to encounter here.

Ben, blissfully unaware of the mini-crisis unfolding in my head, chuckles. "Hey, didn't you guys meet at one of my BBQs a few years back?"

Managing a tight-lipped smile, I muster a nonchalant, "Yeah," while my brain starts racing at playoff speed. "Name sounds familiar..."

"Great, see you in a bit!" Ben calls out, cheerfully oblivious as he shuts the door behind him.

I stand there, momentarily floored, as the reality sets in. Parker Sterling is here, and I'm about to face off with a past fling I thought I'd left, well, in the past.

6

Parker

Strolling through downtown Maple Falls feels like stepping into one of those classic American postcards—quaint shops lining the streets, the scent of fresh coffee mixing with that unmistakable whiff of old books from the corner bookstore.

It's a far cry from the high-octane buzz of city life, but I've got to admit, it's grown on me. Yet, there's a part of me that still craves the rush of an NHL game, the roar of the crowd... yeah, that dream isn't going anywhere.

Tonight, I'm headed to Maple Crust Pizzeria, the town's go-to for anyone claiming to know a thing about good pizza. The place has a laid-back, almost vintage charm, complete with wooden beams and jerseys from local hockey legends on the walls. Definitely my kind of spot.

Despite finding a new groove here in Maple Falls, where my past is more of a quiet murmur than a headline, I still toy with the idea of lacing up for the NHL again. Call it stubborn, but I'm not the type to skate away from a challenge.

As I push open the door to the pizza shop, I spot Ben already camped out at a table towards the back. I weave through the crowd, ready for a night of good food and better company. But then—I see her. Zoe. Instantly, my plan for a relaxing night skids on fresh ice.

There she is, and damn, she looks good.

Ben bounds over with his trademark booming laugh, giving me a slap on the back that almost knocks the wind out of me.

"My man! Fashionably late as usual, huh? We almost started without you!" His wide grin undercuts the mock scolding, his eyes darting quickly to Zoe, clearly curious about the strange way I'm looking at her.

I flash him an easy smile. "You know me – I like to make an entrance."

My attention slips over to Zoe, who's putting on a brave face, her smile a little tight. At her side, there's a bright-eyed kid, about five, gripping her hand—clearly her son and no doubt about it, Ben's nephew.

Looks like we're turning this into a mini block party with a few other parents and their kids are gathered at our table, the buzz of conversation and laughter filling the air.

"Ah, Zoe, let me get you guys reacquainted," Ben continues, gesturing between us with the flair of a seasoned host. "Parker Sterling, meet Zoe, and the young hockey hopeful here, Owen."

"Hey there, champ," I say, crouching down to get on Owen's level, earning a shy nod from him. Standing back up, I extend a hand to Zoe. "And Zoe, great to see you again."

Her handshake is firm, her touch sending a jolt of electricity through me, even as we both pretend this is just a polite reintroduction.

"Yeah, it's been a while since that BBQ, hasn't it?" she responds, her voice calm but hinting at the storm we both know is just under the surface.

"A while, yeah," I reply, our hands parting slowly. The air between us is charged with the unsaid, memories of one night that neither of us has likely forgotten.

Oblivious to the undercurrents, Ben claps his hands, ready to move things along. "Let's get some pizza and make this a proper feast. Parker here has become quite the Vermont enthusiast, haven't you?"

"You know it," I say, my smile broadening as I follow them to our table. As I settle in, catching a quick glance from Zoe, I gear up for an evening of dodging past landmines with a beer in one hand and pizza in the other.

As we snag our seats, little Owen is still clinging a bit to Zoe, sizing me up with those keen kiddo eyes. Figuring it's time to switch on the charm, I lean in with a grin. "So, Owen, I hear you're gearing up to join us at the hockey camp. Ready to skate circles around the big guys?"

Owen peeks up, a trace of shyness still there. But then it clicks—who I am—and his face lights up like a goal light. "You're Parker Sterling??" His voice mixes awe with a serious uptick in volume.

"Guilty as charged," I laugh, throwing my hands up in mock surrender. "Played a few games here and there, maybe scored a goal or two. So, what do you say? Ready to learn some sick moves on the ice?"

He nods vigorously, now fully onboard and firing questions like slapshots. "Can you teach me to skate super fast? What about scoring from the halfway line? Ever done that?"

I dive into each answer with gusto, tossing in a few tales from the ice that seem to make him forget all about being shy. From the corner of my eye, I catch Zoe watching our exchange, her smile soft but her eyes carrying a whole novel's worth of thoughts.

I can't help but keep sneaking peeks at Zoe. Time's done nothing but amp up her allure, and she's absolutely killing it tonight, commanding the space around her despite the emotional armor I can sense she's wearing.

As the pizzas arrive, the table transforms into a feast of grabbing hands and happy exclamations. The aroma of melted cheese and fresh toppings fills the air, and everyone dives in. Owen and the rest of the kids are all giggles and greasy fingers, keeping Zoe plenty busy as she helps him manage a particularly cheesy slice.

While the pizza party is in full swing, Ben leans over, snagging a lull in the chatter to pull me slightly aside.

"Hey man, what's with the tension thermometer rising every time you and Zoe exchange looks? Something I should know about?" His tone is half-joking, half-serious, the big brother antennae up and alert.

I take a deep breath, weighing how much to spill without crossing into the no-fly zone. "Look, it's a bit complicated. Zoe was actually one of the FBI agents involved in that mess a few years back—the whole gambling ring scandal that got me booted from the NHL," I confess, keeping it vague yet pointed.

Ben's eyebrows shoot up, and his "Ohhhh" drags out as he connects the dots. "That explains the frosty vibe," he murmurs, almost to himself, processing the bombshell.

"Yeah," I continue, "We've got some... let's call it 'unresolved history.'" I manage a half-smirk, trying to keep the mood light despite the heavy backstory.

Ben nods slowly, his gaze flickering back to Zoe, who's laughing at something Owen said. "Got it. That's rough, buddy. But hey, she's here now, and so are you. Maybe it's time for some clearing up the air?" He claps me on the shoulder, a silent show of support before sliding back into the bench seat.

I nod, appreciating his understanding.

After we've polished off the last slices of pizza, the energy in the room shifts. The kids, buzzing with post-meal excitement, scramble off to the cluster of arcade games lining the restaurant's walls, their laughter echoing back to us. The parents casually follow, leaving Zoe and me alone at the table. The casual chatter fades, and a more serious tension slides into place.

Zoe's expression hardens slightly as she tackles the topic directly.

"Parker, considering your past involvement in that betting scandal, I'm not going to lie—it makes me uncomfortable to see you in charge of a kids' hockey camp."

I straighten up, feeling a mix of defensiveness and the need to clarify. "Look, I get why you'd think that. But you know as well as anyone that I was never actually charged with anything. I was just in the wrong place at the wrong time, and the media frenzy did the rest. It was all about bad press, not actual guilt."

She folds her arms, her gaze steady and probing. "But when it looks like a duck, quacks like a duck, usually it's a duck, right?" Her voice is calm but pointed, the skepticism clear.

Frustration builds inside me, but I keep my voice even. "In this case, it wasn't a duck. Not at all. I got caught up in something big that I had no control over, and it cost me my career before I could even defend myself."

Zoe looks at me, her eyes searching for the truth in my words. "And you expect everyone just to take your word for it, to trust you with her kid?"

I lean forward, my tone earnest, needing her to believe me. "Yes, because that's the truth. I've worked hard to rebuild my life here, to do something good with this camp. I'm not asking for blind trust, just a chance to prove I'm more than one headline."

Our debate is paused by Owen's sudden return. "Mom, come see this game! You have to try it!" he calls out, tugging at her hand with bright eyes.

Zoe looks from Owen to me, her expression softening with maternal warmth as she stands to follow him. "We'll talk more about this later," she says, leaving a promise hanging in the air.

Feeling a sudden need to escape the growing pressure, I nod to Ben across the room, signaling my departure. Stepping outside, the cool night air hits me, and a heavy sigh escapes my lips. Left alone with my thoughts, I can't help but feel the familiar sting of past accusations shadowing me, even here in Maple Falls.

Tonight was supposed to be simple, fun. But as always, my past is never far behind, making even a simple dinner feel like a replay of old games where I'm perpetually on defense.

7

Zoe

"So, SPILL THE BEANS. What's the real story with Parker after the NHL kicked him to the curb?" I ask Ben, keeping one eye on Owen to ensure he's not about to take someone out with his enthusiastic stick handling.

As we head towards the first full day of practice at the camp, the summer morning air is crisp, painting a perfect scene for what's set to be an action-packed day. Owen is a few steps ahead, his energy boundless as he swings his hockey stick around, pretending to dodge and weave past imaginary defenders. His joyful noises pepper the serene morning, a stark contrast to the quiet conversation I'm pulling Ben into.

Ben sighs, his voice low, matching the seriousness of my question. "Well, it was a mess. Parker was suspected of game-fixing and betting. The NHL took it seriously—suspended him indefinitely while they investigated the whole thing. It was a tough time; he was all over the news, faced a ton of media scrutiny."

He pauses, watching Owen make a pretend goal and raise his arms in triumph. "The investigation dragged on, but in the end, they couldn't pin anything on him. He was cleared of all charges, never formally charged with a crime."

"But," Ben continues, his tone tinged with regret, "the damage was done. His reputation took a hit, and even though he was innocent, the teams were hesitant. No one wanted to take the risk of signing him. Just like that, his career in the NHL... it just evaporated."

Ben exhales deeply, his face clouding over for a moment. "It wasn't pretty, Zoe. Parker took the hit hard—fell into a bit of a spiral, you know? Too much booze, too many late nights with the wrong crowds."

Hearing about Parker's darker days makes me reassess the man I encountered last night—still charming, but with a guarded edge. The contrast between that Parker and the one Ben describes is stark, almost like hearing about two different people.

"He's cleaned up now, though," Ben adds quickly, perhaps noticing my concern. "Moved here, started this camp. Seems like he's really trying to make a fresh start, put all that behind him."

Ben continues, his tone lightening a bit, "I mean, he's really turned things around. I was genuinely worried for a while there, thought we might lose him to his demons, you know? But these past few years, we've gotten a lot closer. After I snagged that work-from-home gig and moved here to Maple Falls, I kept bugging him to come check it out."

I listen, intrigued, as we stroll along the path leading to the camp, Owen's laughter floating back to us as he meets the other waiting kids.

"Finally, he took me up on the offer, came for a visit, and fell in love with the place," Ben says with a chuckle. "Next thing you know, Parker's selling his place in DC, packing up his life, and moving here. It was exactly what he needed, a real reset."

"That's quite the leap," I comment, impressed despite myself. "From city high-flyer to small-town life."

"Yeah, and luckily, he was smart with his NHL earnings," Ben adds. "Made some solid investments along the way. Guy doesn't really need to work if he doesn't want to, but this camp? It's his passion project."

Hearing this, I can't help but feel a grudging respect for Parker's journey. It's one thing to fall from grace; it's entirely another to claw your way back to a place of purpose.

As we enter the arena, filled with the sounds of kids eagerly gearing up for practice, I bring up the topic that's been weighing on my mind.

"There's still the matter of the gambling scandal. He's paying the price for his past decisions."

Ben shakes his head, a frown creasing his forehead. "It's not like that. Parker never really got in with those gambling guys."

I pause, taken aback. I'd been on the investigation team, after all, and everything had pointed towards his involvement. "But I was certain he had been involved. The evidence..."

Ben gives a noncommittal shrug, his expression serious. "Look, I can't say for sure what went down, but from what Parker's told me, and from what I've seen, it seems like the gambling ring might have thought Parker was the one who sold them out. But really, who's to say?"

The uncertainty in his voice adds layers of doubt to the narrative I had been so sure about. Could it have been that Parker was merely a scapegoat in a larger scheme?

"So, you think they set him up because they thought he was a snitch?" I ask, trying to piece together this new angle.

But they were wrong.

I was the one who gave the evidence to the FBI, the one who saw those incriminating documents on his kitchen counter.

But how the hell could I tell Ben that?

"Could be," Ben replies, watching a group of kids run past us with nets and sticks. "Parker's always maintained his innocence, and nothing was ever proven against him, remember that. It's a messy situation, but he's been trying to move past it, focusing on things like this camp."

I nod, processing this new information. The simplicity of Ben's faith in his friend stands in stark contrast to the complexity of the case I remembered.

As we enter the rink, the cool air hits us, a pleasant contrast to the warm summer sun outside. The sound of blades cutting across the ice and pucks hitting the boards fills the arena, infusing the space with an infectious energy.

Ben, ever the host, turns to us with an enthusiastic proposal. "Hey, how about you guys come over for dinner tonight? I can grill something up."

Owen's response from over with the other kids is immediate and enthusiastic. "Yes! Can we, Mom?" His eyes are bright, clearly loving every new experience Maple Falls offers.

I nod, smiling at his excitement. "Sounds great. We'd love to."

As Ben and Parker start organizing the kids on the ice, Parker takes the lead with a booming voice that commands attention yet carries a warm undertone.

"Alright, future champs, let's start with some warm-ups! Remember, even the pros don't skip stretching."

His demeanor with the children is a natural blend of authority and fun, making it easy to see why he's become a beloved coach here.

"Who thinks they can skate faster than me today?" Parker challenges, earning eager shouts and a flurry of hands shooting up.

"I don't know, Park, they look pretty fast," Ben teases, chuckling as he watches the kids swarm around Parker.

"Guess I'll have to pull out my secret moves then!" Parker retorts, winking at the kids, who burst into giggles.

I take a seat in the stands among a few other parents, planning to watch for a while before exploring more of the town. As I settle in, I catch snippets of conversation from a couple of moms sitting nearby.

"It's amazing how good he is with the kids, isn't it?" one mom remarks, unable to hide her admiration as she watches Parker run through drills on the ice. "I heard about his past... all that NHL drama and the betting scandal. It's hard to reconcile that image with the guy out there."

The other mom nods, her gaze appreciatively following Parker as he bends down to help a young player adjust their stance. "Yeah, I know what you mean. My sister filled me in on his history when we signed up. But look at him—he really seems to care about what he's doing. And can we talk about how those hockey pants really do his butt justice?" she adds with a grin, her tone playful yet a bit saucy.

"Right? If coaching doesn't work out, he could definitely have a career in jeans modeling," the first mom laughs, both of them chuckling as they enjoy the view. "Makes you wonder about all those stories, doesn't it? Here he is, turning all that charisma into something so positive."

Listening in, I find myself silently agreeing. Watching Parker now, laughing and skating with a child perched precariously on his back, it's hard to reconcile this image with the one painted by his past allegations.

And yeah, they're right about his butt, too.

The complexities of his situation, the nuances that get lost in public scandal, seem all too relevant now. I keep these thoughts to myself, continuing to observe, the layers of Parker's story adding depth to the unfolding scenes on the ice.

As the ice practice heats up, I tune out the parental sideline chatter and zero in on the rink below, where the real action is. Owen is on the ice, zipping around with the kind of grace and guts that scream 'natural.' Watching him maneuver through his peers with the puck glued to his stick, I feel a rush of pride. He's the main reason we're here—he's got hockey in his blood.

"Nice move, Owen!" Parker shouts from across the ice, his voice booming over the sounds of skates and sticks. Owen beams, clearly thriving under the praise.

Ben, clipboard in hand, is playing the strategist but can't help grinning at the kids' antics. "Alright, team, let's see if anyone can steal the puck from Owen. He's setting the bar high today!"

The challenge sends a ripple of excitement through the kids, their competitive spirits kicking up a notch. They swarm Owen, who dodges with a laugh, clearly enjoying the spotlight.

Amid the fun and games, my stomach tightens with a more serious thought. This summer was supposed to be about fun and hockey for Owen, but it's dangling the daunting task of revealing who his dad is.

And not just to Owen. It could mean letting Ben know that his best buddy and his sister weren't just random faces at a BBQ once upon a time. That's a drama recipe I'm not thrilled to cook up.

Watching Parker interact with the kids, his knack for coaching clear, a part of me softens. Despite his past, he's good with these kids, maybe because he understands second chances better than anyone.

"He's like the kid whisperer, huh?" I comment to a nearby mom, who nods enthusiastically.

"Yeah, who would've thought? Mr. NHL turned Mr. Nanny," she replies with a laugh.

It's hard to square this Parker with the one wrapped up in scandal. And as I watch him now, I'm reminded of the complexities of adult lives—the secrets, the mistakes, and the little truths we hold back to protect the ones we love.

But as Owen skates over to the boards, flashing me a victorious smile, I know this summer is about more than just hockey. It's about truths, past and present, and how I handle them with the people I care about the most. For now, though, I clap and cheer, because Owen's happiness on the ice is the one uncomplicated joy I can fully embrace.

8

Parker

Out on the ice, I'm running the little champs through their paces with some basic drills. Nothing too hardcore, but hey, when you've played in the NHL, you've got an eye for spotting the young guns.

Some of these kids have got it, that natural glide and grit—reminds me a bit of myself when I was their size, not afraid of the big kids or the big goals.

As we break for a quick Gatorade recharge, I pull Ben to the side, nodding towards Owen who's just nailed another drill.

"Man, Owen's tearing it up out there. Kid's a natural—reminds me of, well, a mini-me at that age."

Ben grins, clearly proud. "Yeah, Zoe's been amazing with him. Kid's got hockey in his veins."

That mention of Zoe stirs up a mix of old curiosity and something else. I lean in, keeping it casual. "So, what's the deal with her these days? She settled down with someone? What's the story with Owen's dad?"

Ben's face shifts, a hint of caution there. "That's a bit complicated. Zoe's pretty guarded about it. From what she's told me, the dad was just a fling, never really in the picture."

That hits hard. The idea of Zoe, all fire and wit, handling everything solo because some guy decided to bail? And a great kid like Owen left dad-less? That grinds my gears more than I want to admit.

"Seriously?" I scoff, unable to hide my irritation. "Some guy just skips out on Zoe and a champ like Owen? Not cool, man, not cool at all."

Ben gives my shoulder a squeeze, his tone matching my frustration.

"Absolutely, it's tough. Man, if I ever got my hands on the jerk who did my sister dirty..." His voice trails off, shaking his head in anger. "But hey, look at Owen—he's turned out great, which is the silver lining in all this."

"Yeah," I nod, watching as Owen zips across the ice with a grin plastered across his face. "Let's keep things upbeat for the little guy."

Back on the ice, as the session starts winding down, I notice parents beginning to congregate at the edges of the rink, ready to scoop up their kids. Zoe's among them, her eyes scanning for Owen. This gives me an idea—a chance to put Owen's skills on full display and end the practice on a high note.

"Alright, team! Last drill," I call out, catching the kids' wavering attention. "We're going to do a breakaway challenge. Owen, you're up first, buddy. Let's see if you can get past me and score."

The kids line up, buzzing with excitement as Owen positions himself at center ice. I skate backward, facing him, ready to play the part of the last defender. Owen comes at me full tilt, a flash of determination in his eyes. With a slick fake to the left and a quick dart to the right, he slips the puck between my skates and fires a shot past the goalie into the net.

The rink erupts in cheers from the kids and a few of the parents, including a particularly loud shout from Ben. I skate over to Owen and lift my hand for a high five, which he slaps with a beaming smile. "Great job, champ!"

Turning to the stands, I catch Zoe's gaze. She's clapping, but there's an odd expression on her face—a mix of pride and something else, perhaps a hint of sadness or worry. It's hard to read exactly what she's feeling, but it's clear that Owen's prowess on the ice stirs more than just simple parental pride.

As practice winds down, I skate over to Owen while the other parents start gathering their kids. He's still on the ice, clearly not in any hurry to leave the place where he feels most at home.

"Hey, champ," I start, pulling up beside him. "You really nailed that last shot. You've got some serious moves."

Owen beams, his stick dangling loosely from one hand. "Thanks! I practice a lot at home."

"Yeah? That's great to hear. So, who's your favorite player?" I ask, curious about his hockey influences.

Owen's face lights up, and he doesn't hesitate. "You are! I watched all your old games on YouTube. You're awesome!"

I can't help but grin, genuinely touched. "Is that right? Well, that's quite the compliment, buddy. Thanks!"

We skate a bit as the rink starts to clear out, just chatting about the game. "So, tell me, how long have you been playing hockey?" I probe, interested to know more about how deep his passion goes.

Owen shrugs casually, the smile never leaving his face. "Oh, I don't know. Always, I guess. Mom says I learned to skate not long after I learned to walk. It's always been... easy. I just love playing, love practicing. It's fun!"

"Sounds like you were born to be on the ice," I chuckle, watching his carefree nods and the effortless way he handles his stick, even just coasting along beside me.

"Yeah, I guess!" Owen agrees, then looks up at me with a curious tilt of his head. "Did you always want to be a hockey player when you were my age?"

"Always," I confirm with a nod. "I was just like you—couldn't get enough of the ice. It was my favorite place to be, just like it seems to be for you."

Owen smiles, pleased with the shared connection. "Yeah, it's the best!"

Owen's smile, reflecting our shared passion for hockey, lasts all the way up to where Zoe is waiting at the edge of the rink. Her expression is less than thrilled, a stark contrast to Owen's bright demeanor.

"Time to head out, bud," she tells Owen, her tone firm.

Owen's shoulders slump a bit; it's clear he'd rather stay on the ice a little longer, maybe learn a few more tricks. Reluctantly, he skates off toward the exit, throwing a longing glance back at the rink.

Once he's out of earshot, Zoe turns to me, her expression serious. "Parker, while I appreciate that you've turned things around and you're doing well now, I need to be clear about something," she begins, her voice steady but her eyes wary.

I nod, listening, though a knot forms in my stomach.

"I'm glad Owen has the chance to learn from someone with your talent, but I want there to be some boundaries. I need you to maintain a professional distance with him," she states plainly.

Confused, I respond, "Zoe, I get it, but I only see a lot of potential in Owen. He's a great kid, incredibly talented. I'm just coaching him."

I can tell there's more to it, her concerns digging into deeper soil than just coach-student dynamics. Realization dawns on me, and I rush to clarify any misunderstandings about my past.

"Look, about all that gambling stuff—I was never involved in anything illegal. That was all blown out of proportion."

Zoe listens, her expression unreadable. "Even if that's true, there was still the partying, the womanizing after everything went down with the NHL. That's part of it too."

I meet her gaze, earnest and open. "I'm not that guy anymore. I've changed—a lot. I'm here, fully focused on these kids and this camp."

She pauses, considering my words. "Maybe you have changed, maybe not. But either way, I'd prefer if you keep your relationship with Owen strictly professional."

With that, she turns and leaves, not waiting for a response. I'm left standing there, the chill from the ice creeping up despite the protective boards between us. Her words linger in the air, a mix of caution and unresolved past between us.

Ben slaps my back, breaking through my cloud of post-conversation funk. "Hey, dude, shake it off. How about we hit up The Ice Barrel tonight? You look like you could use a cold one."

I flash a grin, shaking off the residual weirdness from my chat with Zoe. "Yeah, sounds like a plan."

We part ways, and I'm left alone in the gradually emptying arena, gathering the stray pucks and cones. I'm mulling over Zoe's standoffish vibe, trying to piece together her guarded front, when something—or someone—catches my eye up in the stands. Just a shadowy figure, fleeting and elusive.

"Hey, who's there?" I call out, half expecting it to be some kid's parent or a janitor. But no, the figure just melts away, like a ghost scared off by my rugged charm.

Curiosity biting at me, I grab the last of the gear and hustle up to the upper deck. My footsteps echo in the empty space, a stark reminder that it's just me and my imagination—because when I get there, there's no one. Nada. Just rows of empty seats.

"Guess it's just me and the ghosts," I chuckle to myself, shaking my head at my own jumpiness.

Locking up the place, I can't help but feel a twinge of intrigue. Was I seeing things, or is the old arena spookier than I thought? Either way, a drink at The Ice Barrel will do the trick. Nothing like a good beer to wash down a day of drama and ghostly encounters.

9

Zoe

It's been a week since Owen and I landed in Maple Falls, and I'm already marching to the beat of this town's charming, slow rhythm. Today, as I strut down the picturesque streets, lined with vibrant flower baskets and framed by mountain views, it's easy to forget the hustle of DC

I push through the door of the local grocer, greeted by the cheerful chime above. Elsa Thompson, the ever-smiling proprietor, is fussing over a crate of peaches but looks up as I enter. "Hey, Zoe! How's our future NHL star doing?"

"Hey, Elsa," I reply, picking up a basket. "Owen's practically living on that ice rink. Loves every minute." I start grabbing the essentials, quickly filling up the basket and heading to the register.

"That boy is too adorable," Elsa chuckles, her eyes twinkling as she scans my groceries. "You must be so proud."

"Oh, absolutely. And you know what? Back in DC, I couldn't get a cashier to smile at me if I paid them. Here, it's like I'm family or something," I say, half-joking.

Elsa laughs heartily. "Well, that's Maple Falls for you, dear. We like to keep things friendly. Makes the world a bit nicer, don't you think?"

Groceries bagged and goodbyes said, I sashay out, making my way toward the arena. Along the way, I bump into some familiar faces. Mr. Jacobs, the ever-friendly postman, gives me a shout from across the street. "Good seeing you, Zoe!"

Next up, Linda and Nancy from the café, taking in some sun outside their shop, wave and call out, "Hey Zoe, lovely day, isn't it?"

I toss them a grin and a wave back, feeling like a local celebrity in this small town parade. Striding into the arena, I'm reminded why this place might just be the breath of fresh air Owen and I needed—Maple Falls isn't just a town; it's a whole vibe. And I'm starting to dig it.

I arrive at the training camp just as the day's session is winding down, slipping quietly into the stands among the other parents. From here, I watch Owen on the ice, and it's clear he's in his element, his skills sharper than ever. He weaves through his peers with a grace that makes my heart swell with pride. They're deep into a mock game, the intensity palpable even from the bleachers.

Parker skates over to the edge of the rink to address us parents.

"Just so you all know, we're wrapping up the camp with a friendly playoff game against the team from Rivertown," he announces, his voice carrying over the chill of the rink. "They're one of the best local teams, so it'll be a great way for our kids to show what they've learned, put their skills to the test."

I nod, impressed with the setup, already anticipating the excitement of the game. But my thoughts are abruptly cut short by a sharp cry from the ice.

It's Owen. He's down, clutching his leg, and a wave of panic washes over me.

My heart thuds painfully in my chest as I leap from my seat and rush towards the rink.

The other parents murmur in concern, their eyes tracking my swift path down to the ice. Parker and Ben are already at Owen's side, trying to assess the situation as I slide to a stop beside them, my breath caught in my throat.

"Owen, honey, what happened?" I gasp out, my voice tight with worry.

He's wincing, tears brimming in his eyes as he looks up at me. "I—I fell, Mom. It hurts."

"Let me take a look, buddy." Parker drops to Owen's side and gently takes his leg into his hands.

Parker meets my gaze, his expression serious and concerned. "We should probably get him checked out, Zoe. It might be a sprain, but we can't be sure until a doctor looks at it."

Nodding, I help Owen gently off the ice, my mind racing with worry. The fun mock game and the anticipation of the upcoming playoff are suddenly the furthest things from my mind, replaced by a singular focus on my son's wellbeing.

As we rush out of the arena, Parker's already on his phone, barking orders with the urgency of a coach in overtime. He turns off his phone as we reach the parking lot, his face a mask of concern.

"Doc can't get here for an hour," he informs us, slipping the phone back into his pocket.

Owen grimaces, squeezing my hand a little tighter. His discomfort is palpable, and it stirs a fierce protectiveness in me.

Parker looks from Owen to me, his eyes calculating. "Here's the play—I live just a few minutes from here, and I've got a serious first-aid kit at my place, way better than the bandaids and ice packs they have here. We could head over, and I can check him out, make sure he's okay until the doc shows up." He throws in, "I've been around the rink a few times, so I'm no stranger to hockey injuries."

I pause, weighing the options. Parker's place wasn't part of today's game plan, but then again, neither was a potential sprain.

"Alright, let's do it," I decide, more out of urgency for Owen's comfort than any desire for a house tour. "If you think you can help manage his pain, lead the way."

Parker nods, visibly relieved, and carries Owen into my car. As we drive off, I keep a watchful eye on Owen, whose brave attempts to not show his pain only tighten my resolve. Right now, though, Owen's comfort is the only thing that matters.

Parker texts me his address, and I input it into my GPS. It's not long before we're both cruising up a winding road that cuts through the woods surrounding Maple Falls. As we ascend, the trees part to reveal Parker's home—a stunning, modern mansion that looks like it jumped straight out of a luxury homes magazine. My eyebrows shoot up; the guy's living situation is just as impressive as his slapshot used to be.

As we drive, I keep the conversation light with Owen, trying to distract him from the pain. "Just a bit longer, buddy," I reassure him, as he winces and tells me it's his upper leg that's giving him trouble. My heart clenches with worry, every motherly instinct on high alert.

Parker, who's just pulled into his driveway, is already waiting for us. He springs into action, helping Owen out of the car with a gentleness that adds another layer to the complex man I've known. He scoops Owen up with ease, carrying him inside his immaculate home.

The interior is as breathtaking as the outside—spacious, with high ceilings and minimalist decor that somehow feels warm and inviting.

Parker lays Owen down on a plush couch in the expansive living room, chatting with him in a tone that's both fun and soothing.

"You'll be back on the ice in no time, champ," he assures Owen, who manages a small smile despite the pain.

Parker retrieves a well-stocked first-aid kit—more like a professional medical kit—and begins examining Owen's leg.

I watch, somewhat impressed, as Parker gently but expertly examines Owen's injury. His grip is steady as he palpates the area, his eyes focused, assessing for any signs of a more serious injury like a broken bone or a torn muscle.

"Looks like he's got a good range of motion, and there's no obvious swelling that points to a fracture," Parker explains, keeping his tone calm and professional to avoid alarming Owen. "I don't think it's anything too serious, probably just a sprain, but I want to be sure. We should ice it now to keep any swelling down, and then maybe get it checked by a professional if it doesn't improve."

"Looks like a bad sprain, but nothing broken," he announces, and I exhale a sigh of relief I didn't realize I'd been holding. "He should heal up fine with some rest and ice."

Relief floods through me, washing away the tight knot of fear. "Thank you, Parker," I say, my voice filled with genuine gratitude. "I don't know what we would have done without you today."

Parker gives me a reassuring smile, his attention returning to Owen. "Anything for a future hockey star. Let's get that leg iced and elevated, and he'll be trying to score goals again before you know it."

As Parker tends to Owen, I take a moment to look around, impressed by the care he's showing. Maybe there's more to Parker Sterling than the rumors and the rough edges.

Parker heads to the kitchen and comes back with a couple of drinks.

"Here's something cool for you guys," he says, handing me a glass and placing a cup on the coffee table for Owen. We get Owen settled on the couch, flicking on his favorite cartoons. It doesn't take long before the comfort of the plush sofa and the hum of the TV lull him into a nap.

With Owen peacefully snoozing, Parker gestures for me to follow him, and we quietly head upstairs to his office. It's a tastefully decorated space, filled with books and sports memorabilia—a glimpse into the man beyond the rink.

He gently closes the door, turning to explain, "Injuries can spike adrenaline, and that crash afterward? It hits hard, especially with kids."

"Thanks for all of this. Really," I say, feeling a warm rush of gratitude for how he's stepped up today.

His smile widens, and he steps closer. "Happy to help, Zoe. It's no big deal."

But as he steps closer, the room seems to shrink. There's a palpable tension, thick with history and mixed signals. His gaze locks onto mine, that old, undeniable spark flickering to life between us. It feels like no time has passed, like we're those same two people from the barbecue, caught up in a moment.

Without a word, we close the gap. His lips meet mine in a kiss that's soft yet insistent, exploring familiar territory that feels both forbidden and like coming home. The kiss deepens, stirring a cocktail of old emotions and new possibilities, making my heart race in ways I'd almost forgotten it could.

Pulling back just enough to catch his breath, Parker gives me that cocky, knowing smirk that I remember so well.

In that moment, all the complications fade, and it's just us, rediscovering something that, perhaps, was never really lost.

10

Parker

As we lock lips, it feels like striking a match, igniting a firestorm of taste and sensation. Her tongue isn't shy, tangling with mine in a dance that's spicy and sweet—she tastes like trouble, the best kind.

Pressed up against me, her body is a killer combination of strength and curves, making my hands itch to explore every inch.

In between kisses, I manage a cocky grin, "So, this a good idea or what?" The playful challenge hangs between us, electric and buzzing.

She pulls back just enough to catch my eye, mischief sparkling in hers. "The worst," she quips, but her hands tell a different story, quick and deft as they yank my shirt off.

I chuckle, loving her fire, and my hands dive into action, peeling her out of her clothes like I'm unwrapping my favorite gift. Her top goes first, then those tight jeans that do nothing to hide the toned body underneath.

My fingers trace the firm muscles along her stomach, down her legs as she steps out of her denim confines, standing there in nothing but her bra and panties—a knockout view that punches the breath right out of me.

Not one to let a moment go to waste, I slide my hand down, palm pressing against her pussy through the thin fabric of her panties. The heat and the unmistakable damp tell me all I need to know—she's as into this as I am.

My smirk deepens, "Looks like you think it's a pretty good idea too."

Hoisting her up with a confident grin, I carry her straight to the desk. Her laughter rings out, a sound as enticing as the look in her eyes. With a swift, deft motion, I peel her panties down, her eagerness undeniable and my own desire mirroring hers.

She's fully turned on, her breaths quick and shallow, and I can't resist a bit of playful banter. "You seem pretty into this," I tease, watching her reaction closely.

"Shut up and keep going," she retorts with a laugh, her hands tugging me closer, urging me on without words.

I'm more than happy to oblige. My fingers trace down, exploring her sensitively, gauging her reactions. I find her rhythm, my touches becoming more deliberate. I focus on her, listening to the quickening of her breath, the soft moans that escape her as I intensify the pressure, circling and teasing her clit, sliding a finger in and out of her, Zoe's tight walls gripping me.

The tension builds, her body responding beautifully under my hands. Her grip on the edge of the desk tightens, her back arching slightly as she gets closer. I keep the pace, steady and sure, pushing her higher until she crests, a thunderous release that has her calling out, her entire body shuddering with the force of her climax.

Breathing heavily, she looks up at me with those eyes full of satisfaction, a silent acknowledgment of the connection sparking wildly between us.

After she climaxes, I'm nowhere near done. I start showering her with kisses, each one pressing against the smooth, warm skin of her neck, drifting lower with intent. Her moans spill out freely now, a sound that's downright addictive. She tastes like a slice of heaven, and honestly, I can't get enough.

I take my time, kissing down her body, lingering on the soft, sensitive spots that make her squirm and laugh under the tickle of my lips. Each response from her fuels me more, her enjoyment a clear signal that I'm hitting all the right notes.

As I venture further south, the anticipation builds, her breath catching with each kiss closer to her thighs. I pause, giving her a cheeky grin before diving into the real heart of pleasure. The air is charged, her excitement palpable and incredibly inviting.

Positioned between her spread legs, I take a moment to appreciate the view before me—she's completely exposed, vulnerable yet trusting. Then, I dive in. The taste of her is intense, an intoxicating mix that drives me wild. I explore her with my tongue, tracing the contours of her lips that I now know well, each stroke and flick designed to tease out the deepest reactions from her.

I pull out all the stops, mixing slow, agonizing licks with quicker, sharper movements that I know will bring her to the edge. She reacts beautifully, her body arching, her breaths quickening, and when I feel her getting close, I double down, determined to drive her over the edge again.

Her hands find their way into my hair, clutching, guiding with a desperation that tells me just how close she is. And then, she's there—her body tensing, a wave of pleasure overtaking her as she comes hard, her moans loud and unabashed.

As she comes down from her high, I rise up, wiping my mouth nonchalantly. "How's that for a repeat performance?" I ask, my voice dripping with a cocky pride as I lock eyes with her. Her flushed face and heaving chest are all the answer I need, but her smirk tells me she's just as thrilled with the encore as I am.

Now fully in the nude, she reaches down, her fingers wrapping around my manhood with a precision that could only mean trouble—in the best way possible. As she strokes, a pleased sigh slips from her lips, filling the room with the kind of tension you could cut with a knife.

Her response is a wicked grin, and she grabs my ass, pulling me into her with an enthusiasm that leaves no room for second thoughts. The moment I slide into her, everything else fades—it's just her and me and the undeniable fit that has me wondering why we ever bothered with clothes in the first place.

We move together on the desk, finding a rhythm that's half controlled, half wild. Her legs wrap around me, her heels digging into my back urging me deeper. The sight of her below me, hair spread across the desk, lips parted in pleasure, is enough to drive any man wild. And the sound—oh, the sound of her moans mixed with the rhythmic thumping of skin against skin—it's like music, a soundtrack to our reckless abandon.

Driven by the crescendo of her sounds, I thrust harder, each movement more determined as we build toward the climax. Her hands explore my back, occasionally leaving marks that I'll proudly wear as badges of our fun.

As we both race toward the edge, her face is a masterpiece of pleasure, eyes squeezed shut, lips forming an 'O' that could very well be my undoing. Feeling her tighten around me, her body starting to tremble with the telltale signs of climax, pushes me over the edge.

We crash into orgasm together, a riot of sensations that has us gasping, clinging, nearly drowning in the intensity. As I release inside her, the feel of her coming undone under me is just explosive. We're a mess of sweat and satisfaction, and as we collapse into each other, still connected, still catching our breath, I can't resist.

"So, still think it was a bad idea?" I ask with a grin, already knowing the answer.

Lying there, wrapped up in each other and the afterglow of what might just be the best bad idea ever, I can't help but think that if this is wrong, I don't want to be right. The echo of our shared climax lingers in the air, a perfect note of completion to our thoroughly unprofessional escapade.

After we've caught our breath and started pulling our clothes back on, I notice Zoe's got that look—the one where she's miles away, caught up in her head. Clearly, the ghosts of my supposed gambling past are crashing our post-bliss chill. I can't let that slide.

Stepping closer, I place my hands on her shoulders and spin her gently to face me. Eye to eye, I dive right in. "Zoe, let's cut through the noise—I absolutely did not get involved in that gambling mess. Whatever you saw, it wasn't me."

She arches an eyebrow, her arms crossing. "Parker, it looked pretty convincing. Agreements with your signature, terms of bets... ring any bells?"

I shake my head, frustration mixing with a dash of disbelief. "Come on, I didn't sign anything. If there was a signature, it wasn't mine. Maybe a spectacular forgery, but definitely not Parker Sterling-certified."

The room is thick with tension, but I keep my tone light, trying to smooth the edges of this complicated conversation. "I've missed you. And I hate that all this nonsense clouded everything. I wish we'd had a better shot without all the drama."

Zoe's gaze softens, but she's still a cocktail of emotions—hope, doubt, confusion. "Parker, this is... complicated." She bites her lip, hesitating, as if on the verge of saying something pivotal. "If I could fully trust you, there's something important I would tell you."

The weight of her words hangs in the air, my heart skips a beat. "What is it?" I ask, leaning in slightly, the possibility of her revelation pulling at me.

She pauses, the tension palpable, and for a moment, I think she's going to spill a secret that could change everything. But then she sighs, shakes her head slightly, and the moment passes. "It's not the right time," she finally says, backing away from the brink.

"Sure, it's complicated," I agree with a grin, trying to lift the mood. "But hey, I'm here, I'm real, and I'm definitely not the villain they made me out to be. How about giving me a chance to prove it?"

She bites her lip, considering. The air between us crackles with old sparks and new possibilities. I know she's on the fence, but I'm ready to jump through hoops—or over poker tables—if that's what it takes.

"Just think about it. What's life without a little gamble on something good?" I say, hoping to tip her doubts into daring.

As she looks at me, her decision hangs in the balance, and I can't help but hope that maybe, just maybe, she'll roll the dice on us again.The air's thick with unresolved issues, but I decide not to push it. Zoe's got a lot on her mind, and I'm not about to add more weight. We head back to check on Owen, who's still out cold, a little hockey star recharging his batteries.

Slipping back into easy conversation, I nod towards Owen and mention, "He's got some serious moves on the ice. Kid's a natural."

Zoe cracks a smile, watching her son breathe softly. "He really loves it," she agrees.

Feeling like I'm back on safer ice, I add, "He reminds me a lot of myself at that age. The drive, the talent—it's all there."

Suddenly, Zoe's face drops, her smile wiped away as if I'd checked her into the boards. She looks up at me, shock etched across her features like she's just seen a ghost.

Before I can backtrack or throw out a joke to lighten the mood, she's hurrying over to Owen. "We need to go," she says abruptly, scooping Owen into her arms with a swift, practiced motion.

Puzzled, I follow them to the door, trying to figure out what foul I'd committed. "Hey, what did I say?" I ask, hoping to clear the air.

Zoe pauses at the door, Owen still cradled against her. "Thanks for taking care of him, Parker," she says, her tone clipped, all business now. There's a coldness there, a distance that wasn't there a minute ago.

She hustles Owen into her car, the doors slamming shut like a gavel on the conversation. And just like that, they're off, leaving a cloud of confusion behind.

Standing there, I scratch my head, replaying the last few plays. What did I miss? Was it something about the comparison? Whatever it was, it struck a nerve, and now I'm left standing here, wondering what the hell just happened.

11

Zoe

I'm sitting at a corner table in Morning Grind, the local coffee shop, my laptop open in front of me. Owen's at training camp, and I'm in the middle of some highly unorthodox work.

Earlier, when I dropped Owen off, I used the excuse of saying hello to Ben to stop by the camp's office. It was a little sneaky, sure, but necessary. I remember Ben mentioning once that they handled things manually at the camp—no fancy IT setups or check processing companies for them. "The volume of work isn't enough to justify that kind of expense," he'd said. "Besides, neither Parker nor I are too into computers."

With that in mind, I casually rifled through some drawers under the guise of looking for a pen. That's when I found them—checks signed by Parker, waiting to be delivered. Not stopping there, I noticed his agenda open on the desk. It wasn't a high-tech setup, just a simple planner, really.

But it was gold for me. Parker's notes were scrawled all over it, little reminders and messages to Ben, some even on Post-its stuck to the pages. It was clearly his natural handwriting—unmistakable and exactly what I needed.

I quickly snapped photos with my phone, making sure to capture every detail of his handwriting. This was the break I needed, a way to compare the handwriting on those checks to the signatures linked to the suspicious transactions that had put Parker under the microscope.

Back in the quiet of the coffee shop, I open the photos and start comparing them to the scanned documents on my laptop. The morning's coffee buzz around me fades into the background as I zero in on my investigation, determined to uncover the truth.

The screen displays the old gambling case involving Parker, but the lines of text blur as my mind takes a rebellious detour.

In my fantasy, I'm back at Parker's modern mansion, the atmosphere charged with a tension that's almost palpable.

We're standing close in his spacious living room, the fading sunlight casting a soft glow around us. Parker's voice is a low rumble, his words laced with a teasing edge. "You know, Zoe, I always play to win," he murmurs, his breath warm against my ear. His hands are on my waist, pulling me closer, making it impossible to think about anything but the feel of him.

I tilt my head back to look at him, meeting his intense gaze. "Is that so?" I challenge, my own voice breathy but playful. "And what exactly are you trying to win tonight?"

"You," he responds without hesitation, his hands firm on my back now. "A rematch where neither of us loses."

The heat between us builds as he leans down to kiss me, his lips expertly coaxing mine apart in a dance that's as slow and deep as it is urgent. The fantasy is intoxicating, filling my senses, making it hard to remember why we should keep our distance. He slips a finger inside of me, his tongue-tip dancing on my clit, his hands reaching up under my shirt to cup my breasts and...

"Zoe! Order up for Zoe!" The sharp call from the barista yanks me back to reality, and I snap my laptop shut with a click that's louder than intended. My cheeks burn as I realize I've been daydreaming in the middle of a bustling coffee shop.

"Right here," I call back, tucking a loose strand of hair behind my ear as I stand to collect my order. I take my coffee and bagel back to my table, my heart still pounding with the remnants of the fantasy.

As I sit down again, I open my laptop and try to refocus on the gambling case, but Parker's imaginary words echo in my mind, a seductive whisper that's hard to shake off.

I take a sip of my coffee, its warmth a stark contrast to the shivers Parker's imagined touch sent down my spine. Every time I try to concentrate on the facts and figures, my thoughts drift back to what could be—dangerous, yes, but undeniably thrilling. The lines between reality and fantasy blur, leaving me conflicted yet undeniably drawn to the possibilities that Parker represents.

Refocusing on my laptop, I dive back into the complexities of the case that had once seemed like my big break as a rookie. The screen displays scanned copies of the agreements allegedly signed by Parker, agreements that supposedly linked him to some shady mobsters.

As I scrutinize the details, a nagging feeling of doubt creeps in. I remember the rush of landing such a significant assignment early in my career, the thrill of potentially exposing a big scandal. But now, with a sinking heart, I realize I might have been too eager, too ready to believe what was in front of me without digging deeper. Was my desire to make a name for myself clouding my judgment?

Compelled by a need for answers, I pull out my phone and dial Walton Simons, my supervisor. He's always been straightforward, and I trust him to give me the unvarnished truth.

"Walton, it's Zoe. I've been looking over the Parker Sterling case again. Can we talk about the signatures on those agreements?" I ask as soon as he picks up.

There's a pause, and then Walton's voice, always calm, fills the line. "Zoe, that case... it was a mess from the start. The NHL and their lawyers wanted it quiet. They put a lot of pressure on us to just file it away, keep it out of court."

I nod to myself, though he can't see it. "I understand that, but something's been bothering me. The original documents I photographed were just the proposals, so these documents with signatures that surfaced later—where did they come from? I never saw them until after I was removed from the case."

Walton hesitates, his tone uncertain. "Zoe, it's been a long time, and honestly, I'm not sure where those documents originated. They appeared after you recused yourself from the case. Came from one our contacts, I believe. But damned if my memory isn't hazy these days."

"Right, and stepping away meant I wasn't involved when those signed documents appeared. It seems like they were introduced into the file after I left, and no one ever verified them with me," I continue, hoping to underline the gap in the case's integrity.

"Zoe, your decision to step back due to the potential conflict of interest was the right move, given your personal connections. But I admit, this situation with the documents is puzzling," Walton admits, a trace of concern creeping into his voice.

My grip tightens on the phone. "So, you're saying we never confirmed the authenticity of those signatures? We just took what was handed to us?"

"That's about the size of it," Walton admits. "There was a lot of external pressure. High-profile cases like that... they can get complicated."

"I think we need to revisit this, Walton. If there's something off about those documents, it could mean a lot," I suggest, a mix of determination and unease in my voice.

There's a pause on the line, the kind that tells me I'm not going to like what comes next. "Zoe, listen," Walton starts, his tone firmer now, more authoritative. "It's in the past. The case is closed, and digging it up again won't do any good. It'll just stir up trouble, trouble you don't need. It's time to leave it alone."

His words hang heavy in the air, a direct order veiled thinly as advice.

"I'm serious, Zoe. Consider this an order. Drop it. Move on. Focus on your current duties and leave those old ghosts where they belong—in the past. And for the love of God, do something fun! You know what a *vacation* means, right?"

I laugh. "Right."

As I end the call, the weight of the entire conversation presses down on me.

The idea of abandoning my pursuit of the truth feels wrong, but Walton's warning is stark and unyielding. Now, I have to decide whether to follow orders or follow my conscience.

Complicated doesn't even begin to cover it. I hang up, feeling a mix of anger and disappointment. How could I have not seen it? How could I have let my ambition override my duty to dig deeper?

Now, looking back at my laptop screen, the documents seem less like evidence and more like a puzzle missing half its pieces. It's clear I have to revisit everything, question every so-called fact I thought I knew about Parker's case. If there's a chance he was set up, I owe it to both of us to find the truth, no matter where it leads.

Fueled by a newfound resolve, I dive back into the depths of my laptop, piecing together how the NHL swiftly kicked Parker to the curb to deflect the heat from themselves.

The more I dig, the clearer it becomes—Parker was the perfect fall guy, his career sacrificed on the altar of public relations to save the league's face.

As I'm knee-deep in articles and buried under a mountain of legal jargon, I can't help but notice a peculiar guy at the coffee counter.

He orders his coffee but keeps throwing these sneaky glances over his shoulder at me.

At first, I brush it off—maybe he's just curious about the woman who's turned her coffee table into a command center. But his looks keep coming, too pointed to be casual.

Every time our eyes nearly meet, he whips his head around like he's seen a ghost. It's not just odd; it's creepy. I make a mental note of his features—medium build, dark jacket, looks like he's auditioning for a spy thriller with all that shifty behavior.

With Mr. Mystery adding a splash of intrigue to my day, I push even harder on the Parker front. If someone's watching me because I'm digging into this, then I must be onto something. I'm not just going to find the truth; I'm going to grab it by the collar and drag it into the light.

I save my work meticulously, backup on backup—no way I'm letting any sneaky onlooker or coffee shop glitch mess with my findings. As I pack up, keeping one eye on the would-be spy who now pretends to be engrossed in his phone, I'm all steel and determination.

Stepping out of the cafe, I'm ready to chase down every lead, my heels clicking on the pavement like a metronome ticking down to truth o'clock.

12

Parker

My thoughts dangerously drift back to Zoe. Yesterday replays like a too-good-to-be-true highlight reel.

There's something about the way she moved, precise and with purpose, that can drive a man straight to madness. The warmth, the connection—it's all electric, but it's her lips that really did me in.

Picture this: Zoe, on her knees, a mischievous gleam in her eyes that says she knows exactly what she's doing. Her confidence is off the charts as her hands roam expertly, stirring up a storm inside me.

As she leans in, the feel of her lips—soft, eager, insistent—envelops me. That hot, wet warmth of her mouth exploring my most sensitive spots sends pleasure shooting through every nerve. My hands instinctively find her hair, guiding her as gently as my ragged breaths allow.

"Getting all the angles down?" I manage to joke, voice tight with the effort of maintaining some semblance of control.

She pauses just long enough to flash a devilish grin. "Just making sure I ace the subject," she fires back, her voice a sultry promise.

She dives back in with renewed zeal, her tongue and lips in perfect, maddening harmony. Her soft hums and murmurs of approval vibrate straight to my core, each sound dialing up the intensity. She dances along my shaft with her tongue, her hand squeezing my balls just right.

The room fills with the sound of my labored breathing, matched by her quiet, pleased noises. She's in tune with every twitch, every shudder of mine, pushing me closer to the edge with a precision that's damn near artful.

Just as I'm about to cross into bliss, her movements become even more focused, her intent clear. I'm teetering right on the brink, about to let go, when—

But the sharp crunch of gravel outside snaps me back to reality. A car is pulling up my driveway, cutting through the afternoon stillness and scattering my heated daydreams like leaves in the wind. I shake my head, trying to clear the remnants of the fantasy, and stride over to the window to see who's arrived unannounced on my property.

Peering out, I spot a vehicle that's too sleek and official looking to be dropping by for casual reasons. The intrusion grates on me—not just interrupting my personal time, but reminding me how far things have strayed from simple, uncomplicated living.

As I watch the car come to a stop and a figure starts to emerge, I brace myself for whatever comes next, my momentary escape into memory shelved for more pressing, real-world concerns.

As the car door opens, my eyes narrow when I recognize the figure stepping out: Damon Lacroix, a ghost from my past I never wanted to see materialize on my doorstep. The sight of him, poised with that too-familiar smugness, instantly sets my teeth on edge. How he found my secluded haven isn't just alarming—it's a clear invasion of my freshly built peace.

Damon closes the car door with a slick click and strides confidently up to my porch. "Parker," he greets me with a nod, as if we're old buddies catching up rather than adversaries with a troubled history.

"What do you want, Damon?" I demand, stepping out to meet him, making sure he understands he isn't welcome here. My stance is defensive, ready for whatever this might turn into.

Damon strides past me without waiting for an invitation and goes right inside and I follow him in, his eyes scanning the place with a predatory air. He heads straight for the bar, pouring himself a drink as if he owns the place.

"Nice place you've got here, Parker. Looks like you've done quite well for yourself... after everything that happened." His tone is laced with envy and a bitter edge, making it clear this isn't just a friendly visit.

"Cute," I snap back, my impatience getting the better of me. "Skip the niceties. Why are you here?"

He turns to face me, drink in hand, a cold smile playing at the corners of his mouth. For a moment, the old animosity between us sparks like a live wire, charged and dangerous.

"Well, you might be living it up, but the fallout from that FBI investigation didn't go so well for me," Damon begins, his voice low and edged with a cold fury. "When everything went down, my... associates thought I had a hand in blowing our cover. I've been under the gun ever since, trying to clear my name with people who don't listen like the FBI does."

His revelation doesn't bring me any satisfaction. Instead, it's a stark reminder of the long shadows our past actions cast.

"So what?" I ask, not hiding my skepticism. "Why are you here?"

Damon sips his drink, his presence imposing even in the calm serenity of my secluded home.

"Look, Parker," Damon begins, his voice steady and cold, "I didn't just come here to reminisce about the good old bad days or cry over what the streets think of me now."

I eye him warily, my body tense for whatever comes next. "Then what do you want, Damon?"

He smirks, a sharp, humorless gesture. "Straight to the point, I like that. Here's the deal—I'm not just out to clear my name. I want back in, back to the life I had, and you're going to help me do that."

"And why would I help you?" I ask, skepticism lacing my voice.

"Because you owe me, Parker. When everything went down, I kept your name out of some very dirty mouths. I could've dragged you down with me, but I didn't. And now, I need your help to set up a new operation. Nothing too dirty, just enough to get me back on my feet. You're going to lend your respectable façade to help legitimize it. A few introductions, a bit of your shiny reputation... and we both walk away better than we started."

"And if I refuse?" I probe, though I already dread the answer.

Damon's face hardens. "If you refuse, then I make sure everyone knows the skeletons in your closet aren't just myths. I still have connections, Parker, and they'd love a crack at tearing apart the new life you've built here. You help me, and I keep quiet. You don't, and I can't guarantee what happens next."

His threat hangs in the air, heavy and ominous. It's clear Damon hasn't changed; he's the same man who'd do anything to claw his way back to power.

Damon shifts his weight slightly, leaning in closer as if to underscore the seriousness of his proposition. "Here's what I need from you, Parker," he outlines with calculated precision. "First, I need an introduction to some of your high-roller friends from the old days—guys who can invest without too many questions. You make those intros, you vouch for me, and that's it. You're just the middleman."

He continues, his voice dropping a notch, "And it's not just meet-and-greets. I need a front, something clean and shiny that looks good on paper. Maybe funnel some funds through one of your legitimate businesses... like your kid's training camp. Hear you've got quite a bit of cash moving through it these days. Nothing too heavy, just enough to get the ball rolling."

I listen, each word sinking like lead in my stomach. The audacity of his plan churns my gut, but the calm, assured way he lays it out tells me he's thought this through. He believes he's got me cornered.

"And remember, Parker," Damon adds as he steps back, ready to leave, his eyes cold and hard, "it's not just your pretty little setup here that could tumble down. What about Zoe? Owen? How do you think they'd fare with a bit of scandal? Especially with her past entanglement in your case? It'd be a shame if her role got... reevaluated."

His words send a chill down my spine. The threat is clear and ominously pointed not just at me but at the life Zoe and I are trying to build together.

My voice tightens as I confront him, "How do you know about all this? Zoe's role, everything?"

Damon's smirk widens, and he leans in slightly, his voice a low, menacing whisper. "I know everything, Parker. I even know things you don't. Which I'm ready to expose if I need to. People will get hurt."

The threat to bring Zoe and Owen into this mess hits a nerve. Anger flares up inside me, a protective surge that stiffens my posture and hardens my resolve. But I mask it, keeping my face neutral, giving nothing away.

Damon nods, as if satisfied with my silent acknowledgment of his leverage. "Think about it, Parker. I'll be in touch." With that, he turns and walks away, leaving his drink on the sofa side table. Once outside, he descends into his car and drives off, leaving behind a chilling silence.

Standing there, watching the dust settle from his departure, I'm left grappling with the weight of his threats. The idea of dragging Zoe and Owen into the dirty remnants of my past dealings is unthinkable. Damon knows exactly where to press to make me feel cornered, but involving them is a line I can't allow him to cross.

Now, I need to find a way to protect them, to shield the new life I've built from the poisonous reach of old ghosts.

13

Zoe

Sitting at the local bar with Ben, I'm actually enjoying a night off—something rare back in DC. Consider it the one order from Walton that I'm obeying.

Owen's safely tucked away at a buddy's from hockey camp for a sleepover, giving me some breathing room to unwind. It's one of those laid-back evenings that makes you question the high-speed life elsewhere.

As Ben and I catch up over drinks, chuckling at inside jokes, something on the bar's bulletin board snags my attention—an ad from the Maple Falls Police Department. They're hiring. I squint at the flyer, a curious thought bubbling up about ditching the urban jungle for this slice of serenity.

Ben catches my eye line, smirks, and teases, "Eyeing a career switch, or just admiring the local decor?"

I laugh, swirling the ice in my glass. "Actually, I've been thinking. Life here isn't half bad. Beats some of the craziness back in DC."

"Oh really?" Ben leans in, all ears now.

"Get this," I lean closer, dropping my voice for dramatic effect. "Back in D.C., I once left my car unlocked overnight. Next morning? Found a homeless guy and his dog snuggled up in the back seat like it was a five-star suite!"

Ben bursts out laughing, nearly choking on his drink. "No way! What'd you do?"

"Well, I wasn't about to evict them without a notice!" I chuckle. "I woke him up gently, made sure they were okay, and slipped him some cash for breakfast. Got to keep up with the community service, right?"

"Only you, Zoe," Ben shakes his head, still laughing. "That's one way to run neighborhood watch."

Our laughter fades and I take another glance at the hiring flyer. The thought of swapping out car-surprise mornings for peaceful patrols in Maple Falls feels more and more like a plan. "You know, a slower pace might actually suit me," I muse out loud, half-serious. "Might save on breakfast money too."

Ben nods, raising his glass. "Here's to fewer surprise guests and more quiet nights."

I clink my glass against his, the idea of staying in Maple Falls feeling less like a wild notion and more like a tempting possibility.

The familiar ping of my phone interrupts the moment. I pull it out, expecting nothing more than a routine update, but it's an email from a forensic handwriting expert I know back at the FBI. Heart skipping a beat, I open it quickly; this could be the break I've been hoping for.

Sure enough, the email is as significant as I'd hoped. The expert confirms that the signature on the gambling documents doesn't match Parker's known handwriting samples. It's the kind of news that could change everything.

"What's up?" Ben notices the sudden shift in my expression.

I hesitate, then decide to share the news. "It's from a friend of mine in the FBI," I start, my voice low. "A handwriting expert just confirmed that the signatures implicating Parker... they're not his."

Ben's reaction is immediate and visceral. "Yes!" he exclaims, a wide grin spreading across his face. "I knew it! I always knew Parker didn't do those things."

But the weight of the situation keeps my joy in check. "It's not that simple," I sigh, rubbing the bridge of my nose. "I went behind my supervisor's back to get this analysis. If I bring this to light, it could blow back on me—hard."

Ben's smile fades into a frown of determination. "Zoe, you have to go public with this. It's the right thing to do."

I shake my head, conflicted. "Ben, it's not just about doing the right thing. It's about the consequences that come with it."

He leans in, lowering his voice. "Listen, I've got some contacts in sports journalism. We could leak the news to them, get the story out without putting you directly in the spotlight."

The idea is tempting, incredibly so. A chance to clear Parker's name without jeopardizing my career, or my friend in forensics, further. But the risks are enormous. Leaking information, especially of this magnitude, could end my career if traced back to me. Yet, the thought of letting an innocent man suffer because of my fear is equally unbearable.

As I ponder Ben's suggestion, weighing the possible outcomes, the decision looms large. Can I take that step, jump into the unknown for justice? Or is the price of truth too high to pay?

Ben waits expectantly for me to continue, and I find myself on the verge of revealing more than just the forgery. The words almost escape my lips—that Owen is Parker's son. But I catch myself just in time, knowing full well how Ben might react to discovering his best friend and his sister had been more than just casual acquaintances.

"There's... something else," I start, the tension tight in my voice.

Ben leans in, his expression serious. "What is it, Zoe? You can tell me."

I pause, the truth teetering on the tip of my tongue. But instead of spilling it, I shift gears. "It's just... this whole situation could get really messy, Ben. Beyond just my career." I manage to divert the conversation, but my heart pounds with the weight of the unspoken secret.

Before Ben can probe further, my phone buzzes with a new urgency. I glance down to see a text from

Parker.

Need to meet - ASAP

Ben notices the change in my demeanor. "What's that about?"

I lock my phone and meet his gaze, trying to mask my anxiety. "It's Parker. He needs to talk."

Ben nods, understanding the gravity of the situation. "You should go see what he wants. Maybe it's related to what you just found out."

I nod, my mind racing with possibilities and fears. As I stand up to leave, the weight of my decisions—both past and potential—feels heavier than ever. Meeting Parker now could mean facing more than just the fallout of a falsified case. It could mean confronting the entirety of our shared past, Owen included. With a deep breath, I head out from the bar, ready to face whatever comes next.

I slide into my car, punching in a quick text to the Harrisons to check on Owen. A reply pings back almost immediately—everything's peachy, and Owen's having the time of his life. One less worry for the night, but the pit in my stomach doesn't budge.

With Owen safe, I set off towards Parker's place. Thoughts churn through my mind—how to drop the bomb about the forgery, the twisted mess of his so-called guilt, and the nagging secret of Owen's paternity. It's like a storm cloud hanging over what should be a clear night.

Parker's waiting for me as I pull up, standing like a sentinel in front of his house, bathed in the soft glow of the porch light. His posture's tense, a stark silhouette against the dimming sky. Something's off, and it isn't just the usual shadows of our complicated past.

I kill the engine and step out, my heels crunching on the gravel, ready to tackle whatever comes next. But before I can even get a word out, Parker cuts straight to the chase.

"Zoe, we need to talk," he says, his voice tight with urgency. "It's serious."

I arch an eyebrow, pausing mid-stride. "What's going on, Parker?"

He scans the surroundings, a brief glance that tells me he's not just worried—he's spooked. Then his eyes lock onto mine, intense and piercing. "It's about you and Owen. You both might be in danger."

14

Parker

"Damon's on my back, wants to hear from me ASAP," I say, trying to inject a bit of levity into the grim news. "Guy's got less patience than a toddler on a sugar crash."

After I finish spilling the details to Zoe about Damon's nasty comeback tour—threats, shakedowns, the whole nine yards—I watch her absorb the shockwave. It's a lot to take in, and her face says she's halfway between outrage and action mode.

Zoe's eyes flash with a fierce determination that reminds me just why I admire this woman so much.

"We're not letting that slimeball walk all over us. It's time he learned you don't mess with the wrong people. He belongs in jail, and I'll do whatever it takes to get him there."

"Couldn't agree more," I reply with a nod. "Feels like a bad sequel to a movie none of us wanted to see the first time."

Together, we shift into strategy mode, brainstorming like two generals plotting the downfall of a common enemy.

"What if we set a trap?" Zoe suggests, her brain ticking faster than a scam artist's stopwatch.

I grin, liking where her head's at. "Lure him in with what he wants, then snap the trap shut? I like it. It's got a poetic justice feel to it."

"We need to think this through, cover every angle. He's slippery," Zoe adds, pulling out her phone to jot down some ideas.

"Yeah, like trying to nail jelly to a wall," I chuckle, even though the situation is anything but funny. We outline the bare bones of a plan, not getting into the weeds just yet. The finer details would come, but right now, it's about the big picture—taking Damon down before he can do more damage.

As we wrap up, the unspoken risks linger in the air, a cloud of what-ifs that neither of us wants to voice. But the silent agreement hangs between us—this is a team effort, and we're in it to win it.

***

It's two AM, and I'm standing by the window, the only light in the room cast by the moon spilling its glow across the floor. My eyes are fixed on the driveway, where headlights finally sweep across the pavement. Damon's car rolls to a stop, and there he is, stepping out as if he owns the place. He's got that smug swagger that makes my skin crawl, but tonight, it's all part of the game.

Like before, Damon doesn't even wait for an invitation, striding into my house like it's his. He makes a beeline for the bar, pouring himself a drink with an air of entitlement that fills the room like bad cologne.

I can't help but feel a twinge of satisfaction. He's exactly where I want him.

"Parker, I'm glad you've come around to seeing things my way," he says, lifting the glass in a mock toast. "This partnership—it's going to be good for both of us."

I force a smile. "Yeah, we'll see about that," I mutter under my breath as I take a seat across from him.

As he settles into the armchair near the bar, swirling his drink leisurely, Damon lays out his grand plan.

"Here's what I'm thinking," he starts, his tone casual but underlying with command. "Your training camp, it's the perfect front. A little money laundering on the side, nothing too heavy. Just enough to clean what I need. It'll be easy money, Parker. No one will suspect a thing."

I clench my jaw, keeping my disgust in check. "And that's it? I do this, and you're off my back for good?" I ask, trying to sound merely curious rather than fucking furious.

"That's right," Damon assures, with a nod that feels too easy. "You help me out with this, and I'll leave you to your little suburban dream here."

I nod, playing along. "Alright, as long as it means this is the end of it. You get what you need, and then you're out of my life for good."

Damon smiles, a predator pleased with his catch. "Exactly, Parker. You've got nothing to worry about."

"So you admit it then?" I probe, leaning forward, feigning a mix of resignation and interest. "You set me up to take the fall, forged the documents with my name?"

Damon shrugs, nonchalant, his arrogance filling the space between us. "It's the truth," he admits with a half-smirk, swirling his drink carelessly. "Sorry about that, but you know how it is. Bringing the NHL into the mix was just too good a distraction. Helped me slip right out from under the radar."

He offers a smug apology, "Sorry about the career hit, Parker. Nothing personal, just business, you know?" His tone suggests anything but remorse, the words as hollow as the clink of ice in his glass.

"And as a way to say sorry," Damon continues, a sly grin spreading across his face, "I've got something for you. A bit of... let's call it insider information."

I eye him warily, my mind racing. "What could you possibly offer me that would make up for what you've done?" I ask, skepticism lacing my voice.

Damon's grin widens, and he leans in, lowering his voice as though about to share a state secret. "Owen? Cute kid," he says, and I feel a chill crawl up my spine. "He's your son, Parker."

Time stops. I freeze, my blood turning to ice in my veins. The room spins slightly as the weight of his words sinks in.

"What did you just say?" I manage to choke out, my voice barely above a whisper.

Damon leans back, satisfied with the shock on my face. "You heard me, Parker. Owen. He's your son. Surprised you didn't put it together."

The revelation hits me like a freight train. Every moment I've spent with Owen flashes through my mind—the way he looked at me, our interactions, the unexplainable connection.

It all makes a devastating kind of sense now. But hearing it from Damon, in such a callous, offhand manner, makes it all the more brutal.

Damon, seemingly oblivious to the storm he's just unleashed inside me, continues to ramble on.

"And you know, this whole thing with Owen just confirms that you can't really trust that Zoe girl, if you're thinking about it. She's been keeping secrets, Parker."

I force myself to stay calm, keep my face neutral. My mind is racing, but I can't let Damon see the chaos he's stirred up.

"Yeah, well, let's just get this plan rolling and done with," I reply coolly, trying to wrap this up as quickly as possible without alerting him to my true feelings.

He nods, satisfied, and we stand to seal the deceitful deal with a handshake, his grip slimy in its faux friendliness.

"Good decision, Parker. I'll be in touch about the specifics."

With that, Damon strides out, leaving a wake of betrayal and manipulation behind him.

As soon as the door shuts and I hear his car pull away, I turn towards the dark corner of the room. "Zoe," I call out softly.

She steps out from behind the curtains near the couch where Damon had been seated, her face pale, her hands slightly trembling with her phone still in hand. She looks haunted, shaken by the revelations and the role she's just played in capturing them.

"Did you get all that?" I ask, my voice tense, grappling with the betrayal and the sudden expansion of my family that I had no idea about.

As I speak, I head over to the bar and remove the small recording device I'd placed underneath the bar top. I grin as I hold it, knowing I have Damon's defeat in my grasp.

Zoe nods, her voice small, almost lost. "Yes, I got it. Everything."

I take a deep breath, trying to contain the whirlwind of emotions Damon's visit has stirred. "Zoe," I start, my voice firm but controlled, "now you need to tell me why you lied to me about Owen. I need to understand. Now."

15

Zoe

As I STEP OUT from the shadows, the recording still safely in my phone, my mind is reeling. Damon's casual drop of the bombshell—that he knew about Owen—shakes me to the core. How could he have known?

Yet, thinking about it, it makes a grim kind of sense; mobsters like him have their ways and means. They pry secrets out of shadows, use them as leverage. I hadn't planned for this, not this exposure.

I try to shift the focus, clinging to any silver lining. "With this recording, we can clear your name," I say, attempting to steer the conversation towards the positive outcome of our sting.

Parker hardly seems to hear me. His features are etched with a mix of pain and confusion.

"How could you not tell me about Owen?" His voice is a mix of hurt and disbelief, focusing solely on the personal revelation that overshadows everything else.

I bite my lip, feeling the walls closing in as I struggle to explain my side, the decisions that seemed right at the time.

"Parker, I had my reasons," I start, my voice shaky. "Back then, all the stories, the gambling, the lifestyle you were reported to have... I couldn't risk it. I didn't want Owen's father to be a disgraced gambler, a party bro plastered on every tabloid. I wanted to protect him from that."

Parker runs a hand through his hair, his frustration palpable, but as he looks at me, there's a glimmer of understanding beginning to dawn in his eyes.

"I get that you wanted to shield him. I do. But that was my son, my... our son. I should have had a chance to be there, to be better."

The hurt in his voice cuts deeper than I anticipated, and guilt surges through me. I had thought I was doing the best for Owen, but seeing Parker now, understanding the depth of the pain I've caused by my choices, weighs heavily on me.

"I'm sorry. Truly, I am," I say, the words thick in my throat. "I never meant to hurt you. I just... I thought I was doing the right thing."

We stand there, the gap between us filled with years of unsaid words and unshared experiences, both of us grappling with the ramifications of secrets kept too long. Parker seems to understand, a little, why I did what I did, but it's clear that the wound is deep, and the path to healing will be a long one.

I continue, my voice steadier as I try to bridge the distance between us. "I didn't just sit back and accept things. I risked my job, my career, to uncover the truth. Damon forged those signatures, he set you up. I needed to make it right, for you, for Owen."

Parker looks out the window, his profile etched against the dim light, a silhouette of loss and contemplation. When he finally turns back to face me, his eyes are full of a deep, unresolved pain.

"Zoe, I've lost five years. Five years of birthdays, holidays, every day... gone. Five years I could have been there for my son, for you."

I swallow hard, the magnitude of what he's missed washing over me. "It wasn't all bad. The FBI—they took good care of us. They sup-

ported me, even if the job demanded almost all of my time. Owen...
he's had a good life."

But even as I say it, I know it's not enough. Nothing can make up
for the time he lost, the moments he should have shared with us. The
silence that follows is heavy, filled with the weight of what could have
been.

Parker's gaze drifts again, lost in thoughts I can only guess at. The
room feels colder, the space between us wider than ever. I want to
reach out, to bridge it, to start healing the wounds I've unwittingly
deepened, but I'm frozen, unsure if my touch would be welcome.

He takes a few measured steps towards me, closing the gap with a
resolve that seems to steady him. For a moment, he looks like he might
say something, but he stops himself before speaking. His eyes, clear
and earnest, meet mine, holding nothing back.

Parker's eyes drift away momentarily, then snap back with an intensity that pins me in place. The room suddenly feels a lot colder, and he
fills the space with a presence that's both commanding and unsettling.

Finally, he speaks. "Zoe," he starts, his voice steady but sharp with
an undercurrent of raw emotion. "I think it's time for you to go. I'll
be here for Owen—because he deserves the best father I can be—but
you and I? That's a different story."

Confusion and hurt ripple through me. "Parker, what are you talking about?"

He lets out a cold chuckle, and his next words cut deep. "Come on,
Zoe. It was you who turned me in, right? You poked around, stuck
your nose into business that wasn't yours. I pieced it together when
you left that morning and I realized what you'd seen on my kitchen
counter. That's why I never chased after you. And now, after all these
years, my trust hasn't exactly rebuilt itself."

His accusation stings, and my heart races with the urge to defend
myself. "Parker, I'm sorry, okay? I was doing my job, but it was never
about hurting you. I've been trying to fix that ever since."

He studies me, his gaze flicking with a challenge. "You want to make things right, huh?" His voice drops to a mock-whisper, "Prove it. Why should I believe this isn't just another one of your investigations?"

I shoot back, "Because, Parker, I quit playing detective the day I realized my real life was happening without me. I'm here, all in, for you and Owen. Not because it's my job, but because it's my life now. That's my truth."

Parker's hard facade wavers, his eyes searching mine for a hint of the sincerity I feel pounding through every word. The room is silent, thick with anticipation, and I can't quite read his next move. My heart hangs on a thread, waiting for him to decide if we can really start anew.

I take a deep breath, feeling my heart pound in my chest. "Parker, I love you. I know I messed up, and I know it's going to take time to rebuild the trust we lost. But I've never stopped caring about you. You and Owen are my world, and I want us to be a family, to start fresh and build something real together."

I look into his eyes, hoping he can see the sincerity in mine. "I know now what really matters. I'm here, not as an agent, but as a woman who loves you and wants to make this work. I'm ready to do whatever it takes."

Silence stretches between us, the weight of my words hanging in the air. My heart pounds as I wait for his response, every second feeling like an eternity.

Finally, he speaks.

"Zoe, I love you too," he says, his voice thick with emotion. "I think I've loved you from the moment we met."

The words wash over me, unexpected and overwhelming. He continues, "You've been an incredible mother, and I've seen that. I don't want to dwell on the past anymore. All I want now is to be a great father. Owen deserves that. He deserves both of us at our best."

Tears well up in my eyes, happiness mingling with the years of pain and secrecy. "Parker, do you forgive me?" I ask, my voice trembling, needing to hear the words.

He reaches out, gently wiping a tear from my cheek with his thumb. "It's not about me forgiving you, Zoe. It's about us forgiving each other, moving forward from here together."

The simplicity of his words, the depth of their meaning, it all feels like a balm to the years of hidden wounds. "I love you, Parker," I manage to say through my tears.

"I love you too," he replies, and in that moment, it feels like we're finally stepping out from the shadows of our past mistakes.

We lean into each other, and our kiss is a seal on our promises—a new beginning built not on forgetting the past but on understanding and growing from it. In this embrace, I feel a future unfolding, one where the truth no longer divides, but strengthens.

As our lips meet, the kiss eclipses anything I've ever experienced before—it's deep, tender, yet full of pent-up longing and undisguised passion.

Parker pulls back slightly, his eyes searching mine with an intensity that freezes me in place in the best way possible. "Zoe," he whispers hoarsely, his breath mingling with mine, "I want to make love to you. It's never been just about just sex—it's about us, completely, and now more than ever."

Slowly, hand in hand, we make our way upstairs, each step a deliberate pause in the continuation of our newfound connection. In the privacy of the bedroom, lit only by the soft, silvery glow of moonlight streaming through the window, we begin to undress each other.

Each article of clothing removed feels significant, like peeling back layers of the past, getting closer to the raw, vulnerable selves we've guarded for so long.

"You're more beautiful than I remembered," Parker whispers as he traces the outline of my collarbone with his fingertips, his touch as reverent as it is filled with desire.

I laugh softly, the sound mingling with the quiet of the night. "And you're still as charming," I reply, my hands exploring the familiar yet missed contours of his shoulders and back. As our clothes fall away, so does the distance and time that separated us, each touch reigniting memories and forging new ones.

"I've missed this... missed us," I confess as I press kisses along his chest, feeling the steady beat of his heart beneath my lips.

"And I've missed you," he responds, his voice thick with emotion as he leans down to capture my lips again. The room fills with the sound of our breathing, the soft murmur of our voices, and the gentle shift of sheets as we move together.

The moonlight bathes us in its ethereal glow, casting long shadows on the walls and turning our skin to hues of silver and blue. It feels like the world outside has paused, giving us this moment to find each other again, to bridge the chasm of time with the closeness of our bodies.

Climbing on top of Parker, I get the full, glorious view. His eyes, that killer mix of deep green and gray, lock onto mine, heavy with desire and shining in the moonlight streaming through the window. He looks every bit the heartbreaker with his jaw clenched tight, anticipation etching every line of his face.

His chest rises and falls more rapidly beneath me, his abs tightening up with each move I make—a sight that sends my heart racing even faster.

Feeling him inside, filling me up just right, sends a thrill through my entire body. It's like every nerve ending lights up, and the fit? It's like he's the missing puzzle piece. His hands roam over my back then settle on my hips, steering our rhythm into something that's both sweet and fiery.

Our eyes stay locked, the world shrinking to just the two of us wrapped up in this moonlit bubble. He throws me that grin, that damn grin that's equal parts sweet and sinful. His hands slide up my curves, taking hold of my breasts as they bounce in front of him, his thumbs teasing my nipples.

"You're incredible," he breathes out, his voice rough around the edges, charged with raw emotion.

I lean down to kiss him, deep and lingering, filled with all the hunger and promise that's been bubbling up inside me.

The heat between us builds, spiraling into an intensity that nearly knocks the wind out of me. Parker's grip tightens, his touch guiding me closer to the edge. His lips trail kisses along my neck, each one like a spark setting me further aflame.

As the pressure mounts, it builds into a frenzy that consumes me. With Parker's deft moves, pushing and pulling at just the right tempo, I'm catapulted over the edge. The release hits like a thunderclap, intense and all-consuming.

As we come down from our high, everything slows. Our touches turn soft, kisses gentle. Lying there with Parker, wrapped up in each other after the storm of sensations, I can't help but feel like everything's right in the world.

Switching it up, Parker takes the lead, his body shifting as he positions himself above me. His muscles flex visibly under the soft lighting as he moves—a testament to his strength and control. I wrap my legs around his waist, pulling him close, feeling the firmness of his body pressing against mine. As I guide him back inside, the sensation is deeper, more profound than before.

He fills me completely, each slow, deliberate thrust sending a pulse of deep connection through me. His movements are methodical, each stroke drawing a line of fire that ignites every nerve in my body. This isn't just sex; it's love, communicated through the rhythm of our bodies.

Parker's gaze is intense, locked on mine, his eyes dark with passion. His jaw is set, the tendons in his neck standing out slightly as he focuses on the motion, on creating a rhythm that is as much about emotional connection as it is physical satisfaction. His hands, strong and sure, roam over my body, tracing contours, memorizing every reaction I give, every shiver I can't control.

As his cock moves inside me, I feel every detail—the smooth, controlled power of his hips, the way he adjusts his angle just so to hit all the right spots. It's clear in his every move that he's as tuned into my needs as his own, making sure that this experience is something transcendent for both of us.

Between breaths, we trade playful, tender barbs. "Promise you'll keep up," I tease, locking eyes with him.

"I always do," he shoots back with a cocky smile, his movements becoming more purposeful.

As he moves, I feel every detail, every contour. The depth and rhythm he finds just drives me wild, and soon I'm lost in the sensation, pleading with him, "Don't stop, Parker, please."

Hearing my plea, he deepens his strokes, his gaze fixed on mine, filled with an unspoken promise. "Let me take care of you," he says, and the warmth in his voice sends another wave of desire coursing through me.

The build-up is intense, pushing me closer to the edge. As I near the peak, the world narrows down to just the two of us, the connection so palpable it's almost visible. When the climax washes over me, it's earth-shattering, ripples of pleasure cascading through me.

Parker follows soon after, his own release overtaking him. He groans deeply, a sound that vibrates through both of us, and I feel the hot pulse of him as he finishes, the sensation drawing out my pleasure even longer.

When we finally still, breaths mingling, Parker collapses beside me, pulling me into his arms. Our skin is sticky with the remnants of our passion, but it feels right, like perfect pieces fitting together. We exchange quiet "I love yous," the words more than just affection—they're a vow.

"There's still more out there for us to handle," I whisper against his chest, thinking about all that awaits us beyond this room.

"Yeah, but we'll handle it together," Parker assures me, his hand stroking my back soothingly.

"Together," I echo, the word not just a promise but a certainty.

In this quiet moment, with the night deep around us, it feels like we've turned a corner. Whatever challenges lie ahead, we have each other, and that's more than enough to face the future.

16

Parker

THREE DAYS LATER

THE SUN IS SHINING down on Maple Falls, casting a spotlight that feels a bit too intense for my liking as Zoe and I drive to the training camp. You'd think the golden rays would lighten the mood, but there's a tension in the air that even the cheery sunlight can't pierce.

"So, the whole town's buzzing, huh?" I try to keep my tone light, even though my stomach's tying itself in knots.

Zoe shoots me a look, her expression one of worry. "Yeah, it's all out. Between Damon and the forgery, it's another tabloid-headline kind of morning."

I chuckle dryly, keeping one eye on the road and another on the mental preparation for the drama awaiting us.

As the arena comes into view, the real weight of today's agenda hits me. "We've got to square things with Ben," I say, already dreading the conversation. Ben's been closer to me than family, and the thought of how we might have let him down is like a punch to the gut.

"Absolutely," Zoe agrees, giving my hand a quick squeeze—her universal sign of 'brace yourself.' "He's going to feel blindsided, Parker. We kept a pretty big part of your life from him."

"Blindsided is putting it mildly," I reply. "But hey, if anyone can handle a soap opera twist, it's Ben, right? We'll just lay it all out. Honesty is the best policy, or however that saying goes."

Zoe smiles weakly, appreciating the effort to keep things light. "Just like snapping a twig, quick and clean."

I laugh. "And hopefully he doesn't attack us with this now-broken twig…"

As we park and make our way to the arena, I can't help but feel like I'm walking into the lion's den, albeit armed with truth and a dash of hope.

"Time to face the music, and hopefully, it's more of a forgiving tune," I say.

As Zoe and I park at the arena, I see Ben right there with Owen, probably sharing some pre-game wisdom. Zoe bends down to Owen, giving him the nod to go on ahead. "Go on, superhero, we need a minute with your Uncle Ben."

Owen, oblivious to the brewing storm, jogs off with his hockey stick, probably dreaming of scoring game-winning goals. As soon as he's out of earshot, I brace myself for the inevitable showdown with Ben.

I barely have a moment to prepare a greeting before Ben marches over and serves up a not-so-friendly punch right to my jaw. It's not a haymaker, but it definitely rings my bell.

Rubbing my jaw, I shoot him a grin, "Hey, Ben, if you were looking to start a boxing training camp too, you could've just asked."

Ben isn't amused. "That's for what you did with my sister," he growls, eyes still burning a bit.

Zoe steps in, playing referee. "Cool it, Ben. We're good now, really. No grudges."

Ben shifts his weight, eyes darting between Zoe and me, sizing up the situation. He finally fixes his gaze on me, searching for sincerity. "You gonna be there for Owen? For real this time?"

"Absolutely," I respond without hesitation. "Nothing's more important to me."

Seems my answer hits the right note because Ben's expression softens, and he claps me on the shoulder—still hard enough to count as round two but friendlier. "Alright then," he concedes. "Time to have a little chat with Owen. Together."

"Lead the way," I say, following him into the arena with a mix of nerves and anticipation. It feels like stepping into a new league, one where truth plays better than any defense I've ever faced.

As we step into the arena, the crisp snap of cold air and the familiar sound of skates cutting through ice hit me. There's Owen, center ice, moving like he was born with blades on his feet. His sprain from the other day ended up being nothing – one night of rest and he was right as rain.

I pause for a second, just taking it in. That's my kid out there—suddenly, the reality of it punches me right in the gut, but in a good way.

Watching him weave across the ice with the kind of ease some folks have walking, I can't help but puff up with pride. "Look at him go," I say, half to myself, half to Zoe. It's like watching a mini-pro, and heck, that's my blood right there!

Zoe waves to get Owen's attention. "Owen! Skate over here, buddy. We've got some big news to share!"

"OK!" His voice rings out, clear and vibrant across the ice. He pivots and starts heading our way, his skates slicing a sharp, confident path.

As he approaches, a strange sensation wells up—part pride, part nerve. For a moment, my usual cool falters, and I feel a suspicious sting in my eyes. Tears? No way, must be the ice.

Watching your son zoom over with the world's biggest grin, about to drop a life-changer on him, would make any man's eyes... well, you know, react to the cold.

Epilogue

ZOE

ONE YEAR LATER

A year has flown by since everything turned on its head, and here I am in my Maple Falls Police Department uniform, patrolling the charming streets of our little town on a gorgeous summer evening.

The sun is setting, casting a warm glow over the quaint downtown, and I'm wrapping up my shift before heading off for the night.

As I walk past the tidy rows of shops along Main Street, I nod and exchange hellos with familiar faces. There's Mr. Walsh, watering the flowers outside his bookstore.

He gives me a wave and big, warm smile. "Evening, Officer Zoe!" he calls out cheerfully.

"Good evening, Mr. Walsh! Keeping those petunias hydrated?" I reply, my tone light and friendly.

Just a few steps further, I pass by the Maple Falls Café, where Sara is pulling in the outdoor seating for the night. "Hey, Sara! Closing up?"

"Yep, just about done for the day. How's the beat, Zoe?"

"Quiet as ever, thankfully," I chuckle, continuing my walk.

Reflecting on the past year, it's almost surreal—resigning from the FBI, watching Parker negotiate his return to the NHL, and settling into life here in Maple Falls. Parker and I have even started discussing getting a place in New York, where he's likely to play, but for now, this small town feels like home.

The streets of Maple Falls are peaceful, and as I finish my patrol, the familiarity and warmth of this community remind me why I made the choice to stay.

As my shift wraps up, I'm practically bouncing on my toes with excitement. It's the big night—Parker and Ben's training camp showdown against Rivertown, and I wouldn't miss it for the world. This friendly "playoff" game has quickly turned into the highlight of the summer, a tradition that's got the whole town buzzing.

I hustle back to the station, quick to ditch the uniform for something a little less formal and a lot comfier. Slipping into my favorite Maple Falls tee and jeans, I feel my shoulders relax—the night's just beginning, and I'm ready to dive in.

The sunset's painting the sky in strokes of orange and purple—perfect game night vibes. Reflecting on the past year, I can't help but smirk a bit. Sure, diving behind my supervisor's back to dig up the dirt on Parker's case wasn't exactly by the book, and yeah, it nearly cost me my career.

But, my old boss decided to let bygones be bygones. And honestly? All that drama just hammered home how much I needed a change from the DC grind. Wasn't exactly looking to play the role of a scandal-plagued FBI agent for the rest of my days.

Now, as I approach the arena and hear the roar of the crowd, the crack of hockey sticks, I'm grinning ear to ear. Moving to Maple Falls, stepping into this simpler, sweeter life—it's been a game-changer. Here, under the glow of the arena lights, cheering alongside Owen and watching Parker do his thing, I know I've scored big.

No second guesses, no what-ifs. Just the open ice of a new life where I call the shots. Tonight, like every night from here on out, I'm exactly where I need to be—front row, center ice, living the dream.

I breeze through the arena doors and instantly, the electric vibe of game night washes over me. The stands are bursting at the seams—looks like the whole town decided to show up. Ever since last year, what used to be a low-key scrimmage has turned into the social spectacle of the season, complete with a post-game BBW bash that's the talk of both Rivertown and Maple Falls.

Down on the ice, Parker and Ben are in their element, rallying the troops with that last-minute coach magic. After smoothing over their rough patch—yeah, the whole saga of Parker and me—those two are thick as thieves again, coaching these kids like they were born for it. And there's Owen, my boy, holding down center like a champ, looking every bit the mini-version of his dad.

I throw a wave their way and snag some grins from Parker and Owen. Their matching smiles? Total heart-melters. I scoot into my seat next to some familiar faces from around town.

The puck hits the ice, and the game is on. The crowd goes wild, every goal, every save ramping up the cheers to near-deafening levels. Between the shouting and the buzz, it's like we're at the center of the universe right here in Maple Falls.

Sitting here, yelling along with my friends, feeling the pulse of my hometown, it's clear—I nailed the decision to plant my roots here.

The game is absolutely electrifying, keeping every single soul in the stands on the edge of their seats. The kids are zipping across the ice, their skates carving sharp lines in the rink, and the puck is practically on fire, ricocheting from one stick to another. The goalies are putting on a clinic, snatching saves out of thin air, and every near-miss puck has the crowd alternating between cheers and groans.

Then, in the final stretch, Owen takes the puck like it's his destiny. He maneuvers through the defense as if he's dancing, not skating. With a slick flick of his wrist, he sends the puck sailing straight into the goal—bam, game-winner! The crowd goes wild, absolutely loses it, and Owen's teammates swarm him like he's a rock star.

After the euphoria settles, Parker steps up for his victory speech, mic in hand, all smiles and sparkling eyes.

"Thanks, everyone, for turning up and turning this game into a blockbuster night. Watching these kids tonight, I'm reminded why Maple Falls rocks. You've all opened your hearts to me and my family, and I can't tell you how much that means. We've had our ups and downs, but thanks to you, Maple Falls is home. Here's to more games, more good times, and more nights like tonight!"

The cheers that follow could raise the roof. As the clapping fades, I take a moment to soak it all in. Parker's transformation from scandal-headline to hometown hero is complete, and seeing him embraced like this just gives me all the feels.

And then there's Damon, that sleazeball. My final act at the FBI was making sure he got a one-way ticket to a cell. Knowing he's locked up adds an extra dash of sweetness to the evening.

But enough about that—party time is calling! The arena's shifting from sports venue to party central, and I'm ready to dive into the fun. Tonight, it's all about good vibes and great music. Maple Falls isn't just where I hang my hat; it's where my heart is.

And tonight, it beats loud and proud for this little town.

The game wraps up and we all spill out into the park next to the arena, where the setting sun is turning everything into a golden-hour dream scene. Ben's at the grill, showing off skills that have definitely leveled up over the years. He's flipping burgers like a champ, and the sizzle sounds almost as good as the applause in the arena.

I spot Owen and Parker soaking up the victory vibes and make a beeline for them. Owen barely gets a warning before I'm all over him with congratulatory kisses.

"You were just spectacular out there, champ!" I cheer, planting one last smooch that earns me an eye roll.

"Mom, seriously!" Owen groans, doing that adorable embarrassed thing kids do when their parents show them up with love in public. He squirms out of my grasp and bolts to his friends, leaving me chuckling after him.

Turning to Parker, I catch that proud, happy glint in his eyes and pull him into a quick, celebratory kiss. "And you, Coach, knocked it out of the park today," I tease with a grin.

Parker leans in, a sneaky smile playing on his lips. "Babe, I've got some news," he whispers, excitement bubbling under his words. "Looks like the New York Rangers want to sign me."

I let out a squeal that probably turns a few heads, but who cares? "That's amazing!" I throw my arms around him, squeezing him tight enough to make sure he's real.

We hug it out right there, with the party buzzing around us. It's a moment of pure, exhilarating joy. The buzz of New York might be on the horizon, but right here, right now in Maple Falls, it feels like everything's clicking into place.

As we stand there basking in the excitement of his news, I notice a shift in Parker's expression—a flicker of something serious crossing his face. My smile fades a bit, replaced by curiosity. "Hey, what's up? You look like you've got something on your mind," I ask, scanning his eyes for clues.

He gives me a small, mysterious smile and gestures towards the edge of the park. "Come with me for a sec," he says, taking my hand and leading me away from the crowd. We walk over to a big tree that stands like a sentinel on the far end of the park, giving us a secluded spot with the party lights twinkling in the distance.

Under the branches of the tree, Parker turns to face me, his eyes deep with emotion. "Zoe," he starts, his voice soft but clear, "this past year, having you and Owen in my life... it's changed everything for me. I've never been happier, never been more sure of anything." He takes a deep breath, and his next words come straight from the heart. "I love you, Zoe, more than I ever thought possible. And I want us to be a family, officially, forever."

Before I can even process the wave of emotions his words unleash, he reaches into his pocket and pulls out a gorgeous ring. Going down on one knee, he holds it up to me. "Will you marry me, Zoe?"

Tears of joy spring to my eyes, and a laugh escapes me in a burst of happiness. "Yes! Yes, a thousand times, yes!" I exclaim, slipping my hand forward so he can slide the ring onto my finger.

As we embrace, the joy overwhelming, I pull back slightly and say with a mischievous grin, "Well, since we're sharing surprises..." I reach into my purse and pull out a small item, handing it to him. It's a positive pregnancy test.

Parker's eyes widen, a look of pure elation overtaking any other emotion. "Really?!" he gasps, and as I nod, his happiness mirrors mine. He lifts me off the ground in a tight hug, overjoyed.

"We're going to have a baby," I whisper into his ear as he sets me down, and we share a kiss, filled with love and promises of new beginnings.

Hand in hand, we walk back to the party, ready to share our double dose of good news. The night echoes with our laughter and the cheers of our friends as we tell them about our engagement and the baby on the way.

It's a perfect ending to a day full of victories, and as we look into each other's eyes, we know it's just the start of our happily ever after.

THE END

A NOTE FROM THE AUTHOR

Dear Reader,

Thank you for reading this short book. I hope you enjoyed it!

And if you liked Parker and Zoe's journey, you'll *love* 'Pucking My Next-Door Enemy'! It really is a great book.

A Sneak Peek is just one page away...

Quick favor: Please leave a review for this short romance to share your thoughts. Your words can help others discover their next read! Scan the QR code below with your smartphone's camera to go directly to the review page—no scrolling needed!

Scan me

Thank you so much.

Let's continue our literary adventures, one page at a time.

Love,

Livvy

Pucking My Next-Door Enemy

A Brother's Best Friend Second Chance Romance

Mistake #1: Hooking up with a stranger when my life's in danger.
Mistake #2: Not recognizing he's my brother's best friend whom I've always hated.
Mistake #3: When I do know, becoming his fake fiancée *anyway*.

Targeted by a dangerous gang because I know military secrets,
I'm fleeing to my small town to hide.

Traveling in disguise, I stop to find a stress-relief partner.

Whoah, do I find him—
a tall, hot, brooding hunk with a killer smile and a body to die for
who looks at me with hunger and devotion
as he pleasures me like no one ever has before.

Once at my brother's, I discover the "stranger" is his neighbor,
billionaire puckster, and lifelong best friend Mike Hunter.

I didn't recognize him because, well,
the little Mikey I knew is now so very, very big (*wink*).

When my enemies close in, Mike steps up
and falsely declares himself my fiancé to protect me.

As we pretend, the reasons why we shouldn't be together start to fade away.

So maybe... just maybe... my only *real mistake* has been hating him...

——

Trigger warning: This book is a spicy standalone hockey romance with no cliffhanger. But in their journey to a HEA, Mike and Eve do face some violent characters. Please be mindful of your comfort level before reading it.

Scan this QR Code and Get Your Copy of "Pucking My Next-Door Enemy" Now!

Scan me

Flip the page and start reading!

Pucking My
Next-Door Enemy

A BROTHER'S BEST FRIEND SECOND
CHANCE ROMANCE

1

Eve

"IS THIS SEAT TAKEN?" a voice asks confidently.

I turn on the bar stool and look the man up and down slowly. Tall, blonde, not bad looking, wearing a designer suit and tie.

He looks like a douche.

"Yes, I'm waiting for someone," I reply as I look away.

Two weeks ago, I bought a new car, loaded it down with some of my personal belongings, and Diesel and I started a trek across the country to return to my hometown after some men from the Tambov Gang, the Russian Mafia, showed up at my house.

My Pitbull, Diesel, is a trained military/police dog. I had a similar incident a few years ago and my mentor at the time hooked me up with a rescue group who trained dogs as service animals. Diesel quickly became my protector and best friend.

I don't want to be found, so Diesel and I drove from California up and crossed the border into Canada before dipping back down to the United States by way of Michigan. I'm using cash and burner phones, my regular phone has as much advanced security protection on it as it can have, but when dealing with these types of people, you can never be too careful.

I am about eight hours from my hometown of Legacy right now and that's where I'm headed to stay with my brother for a bit. Our parents died in a car accident when I was sixteen and my brother took care of me until I turned eighteen. We used to be really close, but life took us away from each other. I have been here in Detroit for the last few days. I started talking to a guy named Mark on Bumble and he is supposed to be meeting me here.

Because of my background and job, I tend to get to dates at least thirty minutes earlier. In doing so, it gives me the opportunity to pick my seat with a view of all entrances and exits, while also scoping out the place and the people in it. I can never be too careful when it comes to meeting someone online, for obvious reasons as a woman, but also because the Tambov Gang isn't the only group of derelicts who would love to get a hold of me.

This man is not him. Not even close.

I like my men not in the douchebag flavor and he screams it.

"I'm that someone."

"No, you're not."

"I could be."

There's a lot of chaotic noise behind us as a group of six men walk into the bar. I glance back briefly noticing they're rowdy and annoying.

The blonde man in a suit takes a step forward, putting his hand on me.

"I'm sorry," I purr as I grab his wrist. "Did I say you could touch me?"

He laughs awkwardly, clearly thinking I'm playing hard to get.

"You don't have to say the words, babe, when you wear a dress like that. It's obvious you're looking to be touched in all the right places."

Entitled. Douchebag. Creep.

I laugh as I tighten my grip on his wrist, about to engage him in a wrist lock when someone knocks into me hard from behind.

The douchebag rips his arm away. He takes a step toward whoever bumped into me and puffs up.

I turn around and fall into a pair of light, soft green eyes.

Holy Hell, are those real?

He kind of looks like my Bumble date. Damn, that's good timing.

My stomach flips and I suck in a breath as he puts both hands on my arm. Electricity shoots through me.

"Oh man, I am so sorry," a deep baritone voice says, barely audible over the noisy bar.

"Are you Mark?"

"Yes, how are you? Again, I'm sorry. We're a little wild today."

"No problem," I smile. "Have a seat."

The blonde in a suit shoots me a dirty look, removes his grubby paw from my arm, and walks away in a huff.

"Who was that guy?"

"Someone who didn't take no for an answer."

"Let me buy you a drink, gorgeous," he smiles as he gestures toward my almost empty beer.

"Sure, but only if you promise to make it worth my while."

"Oh, I have no doubt that it will be worth your while."

"I love a confident man."

This man is way hotter than his profile pictures online. He's like a six-foot-six wall of muscle. He's got shaggy blondish-brown hair and a goatee.

"What brings you in here tonight?" he asks before he hails the bartender and orders us both drinks.

"You," I reply flirtatiously.

He glances back at me and chuckles. "Lucky me."

"Are you and your friends celebrating something or are you always the life of the party?"

"Both. You look like you could be trouble."

"I am."

Our eyes lock onto each other and I get lost in his sexy, soft green eyes. A smile tugs at the corner of his mouth.

"I can handle that challenge."

"That's what I'm hoping for."

"You're absolutely breathtaking," he says as he turns toward me and takes a long pull from his beer bottle. "Can I kiss you?"

I laugh as I lean toward him and kiss him instead. "Asking ruins the mood," I reply as I pull away from him.

He pulls me right back into another kiss. This time, I can feel the warmth flooding my core as his hands go up to my face.

"I have a room upstairs; do you want to continue this there?"

"Lead the way, Romeo."

I stand, he takes my hand and leads me out of the bar. We go to an elevator and as soon as the doors close, he's pulling me into a hot kiss.

The elevator dings softly as we reach his floor, and he leads me down the hallway to his room. As he fumbles with the key card, I can feel the anticipation building in the air between us.

The door swings open, and he pulls me inside, not wasting a moment before pressing me against the wall in another searing kiss. The room is dimly lit, the only source of light filtering in from the city outside, casting long shadows across his face.

His hands are on my hips, firm, but he's hesitant to explore anymore.

Guess I'll take charge then.

My hands go down to his pants, unbuttoning them quickly. He takes the hint and his mouth moves down to my cleavage, exploring hungrily while his hands move down to grab my ass cheeks.

Atta boy.

I moan as I unzip his pants and yank them down. He removes them the rest of the way while also continuing to kiss me.

That's talent.

He hikes up the hem of my little black dress and reveals that I'm not wearing any panties. His eyes find mine before he grins back at me. He drops to his knees in front of me before he spreads my thighs apart.

Yes!

He buries his face in between my legs, moaning as he gets his first taste of me. The vibration sends tingles all over my body and I gasp.

My hands find their way to his hair, tugging gently as he licks and sucks on me, driving me wild. The feel of him is intoxicating.

My breathing quickens as he explores further, his tongue darting in and out, teasing me to the brink.

"You taste so good," he groans into my wet folds, making my heart race. "I could spend all night down here."

The heat between my legs is building, and I know I won't be able to hold back much longer.

He stands up, kisses me, and cups my butt, lifting me up. I wrap my legs around his waist as he guides himself inside me, filling me.

"Yessssss," I breathe.

I grip his shoulders tightly as I grind down on him.

His eyes lock with mine as he thrusts slowly, our bodies moving in perfect harmony.

A low groan escapes my lips as he picks up the pace, each thrust deeper than the last. My breath catches in my throat as the pleasure builds, the tension within me coiling tighter and tighter.

He leans down and kisses me softly, his breath warm and ragged against my lips. His touch is electric, and his hands roam over my body, sending shivers down my spine. He knows exactly where to touch with his hands, and his mouth, it's like he's the conductor of my body.

He carries me to the bed.

"Spread your legs," he commands, his voice low and gravelly. I comply, eagerly opening myself up to him. He takes a moment to take in the sight of me, lying there naked and exposed, before he crawls up my body, his eyes never leaving mine.

His lips meet mine in another passionate kiss, his hands exploring every inch of my skin. I arch my back, wanting to feel more of him against me, and he complies, positioning himself at my entrance.

He enters me again, this time slowly before he hits my G-spot.

"There it is," he breathes.

I don't know that I've ever had a man know when he hits that spot, at least not that they've voiced.

Fuck.

I let out a gasp as he hit just the right spot, my entire body trembling with pleasure.

"Take it, baby, take it all," he urges, thrusting into me deeper and harder with each word.

He pumps his hips faster and faster, sending electric sparks through me. I can't help but moan, my body responding to his every touch.

"That's it, take it, take it all," I whisper back, my voice barely recognizable as my own.

His hands grip my thighs. His body moves with a power and intensity that sends shockwaves of desire through me. I want him to take me higher, to push me over the edge and into the abyss of pleasure.

He picks up the pace, his thrusts becoming harder and faster, hitting my sweet spot over and over again. The room is a haze of sensation, the city lights dancing in the shadows as the sounds of our passion fill the room.

Then, suddenly, everything comes to a head as I cry out, arching my back and clinging to him as the most intense orgasm of my life takes over. He continues to thrust into me, his own release building.

With every swift thrust, he takes me to the edge, and I can feel it coursing through me. My orgasm is building up within me, like a volcano about to erupt. I cling to him, my nails digging into his back, unable to control myself.

"Oh, God," I moan, my voice trembling as I surrender to the wave of pleasure flooding over me. The whole world fades away, and all that exists is him and me, connected in the most intimate of ways.

He keeps thrusting, riding out my climax, pressing into me with every powerful stroke. It's intense, it's beautiful, and it's ours. His eyes stay locked with mine, the heat of them burning into me, reflecting my own desire.

He lets out a primal growl and collapses on top of me, spent and panting.

"That was incredible," I whisper, finally able to catch my breath. He kisses me softly, tendrils of warmth still pulsing between us.

"Are you okay?" he asks, his voice soft and concerned.

I smile up at him, a warm feeling spreading through me. "Better than okay," I reply. "I've never felt so alive."

"Good, we're feeling the same vibe."

He slowly pulls out of me, moves to the side, and pulls me into him.

Normally, I would bail after sex. I'm not the cuddly type at all.

I can't be, especially now. One night stand with a hot guy that I'll never see again, that's all this can be. But for now, I'm going to pretend like I didn't write a computer program for the military that has caused the Russian Mafia to come after me so that they can get classified information.

I'm putting this sweet man's life in danger by even being with him tonight.

I used a fake name on the dating site, so hopefully he doesn't suffer for this one night of sweet release.

I feel so safe right here.

Damn it, it's that really good orgasm afterglow that has me feeling like he'll protect me from dragons.

You can protect yourself, girl. Get out of here.

"Damn, I am worn out," he chuckles. "Usually, I have way better stamina than this."

"That's what they all say," I giggle.

"Is that so? Let me get a ten-minute power nap and then I'll make your legs shake even more than they already are."

"All talk."

He chuckles and pulls me into him. "It's a promise."

He closes his eyes and within a few minutes, he's sound asleep.

It's really annoying how men can do that.

My phone buzzes with a notification. I have a new message on Bumble. I open the app to see that Mark has messaged me.

What?

> Hey, I'm really sorry I missed our date. I think I have COVID, I've been asleep for the last twelve hours. Raincheck?

Who the fuck is this man if he's not Mark?

Shit, Eve, shit. How did you let this happen?

I move and when he doesn't notice I remove myself from the bed. I straighten my clothes quietly leaving his room.

I immediately go to the shower, and turn the spray on as hot as it can go before, I climb in.

Was he one of Ivan's guys?

No, if that were the case I'd be dead. He'd have taken the many chances I'd given him to catch me off guard.

Was that just dumb luck that I ran into a hot guy with an incredible dick?

That guy seemed pretty great, he definitely knows what he's doing with that dick and mouth, but it can't be anything else.

I have to get to my brother's house and hide out. Ivan, the man chasing me, won't know to look for me there and it's my only chance at staying alive.

The only chance Mark, or whatever his real name is, has at staying alive.

I can't bring him into this no matter how bad my body wants to go back to him.

Scan this QR Code and Get Your Copy of "Pucking
My Next-Door Enemy" Now!

Scan me

SHADY SHOT BY MY SECRET BABY DADDY